LOYAL AFFECTION

REMEMBER WHO YOU LOYAL TO

JAHZAEVION "J CLIP" MOSLEY

authorHOUSE®

AuthorHouse™
1663 Liberty Drive
Bloomington, IN 47403
www.authorhouse.com
Phone: 1 (800) 839-8640

This is a work of fiction. Names, characters, places and incidents either are the
product of the author's imagination or are used fictitiously, and any resemblance to
any actual persons, living or dead, events, or locales is entirely coincidental

Published by AuthorHouse 08/07/2019

ISBN: 978-1-7283-2238-4 (sc)
ISBN: 978-1-7283-2237-7 (e)

Library of Congress Control Number: 2019911350

Prologue

Starring into the bathroom mirror looking back at myself, wondering who the hell is she. What am I doing, and how did I get here? I'm so overwhelmed with stress and anxiety not knowing what's next. How can one man leave me so in shambles.

"I hate you Kevin" I whisper aloud

I can't believe I just let him walk out my life like that, I should've done more. Why, why, why, It's not fair. I will never let another man have this much power over my emotions again I hate how I feel right now. I miss him so much, I love him so much, I can't be without him. He doesn't even want me though.

My own thoughts consume me with a sudden bitter sorrow and I flop down like a rag doll on the cold depressing floor and cry.

Lost in thought I envision myself stabbing Kevin in the eye and cutting his heart out of his chest; then rushing him to ER just to be there for him, love him and take care of him. Why do I think about him so damn much. I'm so stupid for loving him, never again. I was loyal to him, I only gave him my love and affection. "Loyal affection what have you done for me, ever" I mumble with frustration and anger.

Being loyal got me looking stupid and heart broken; not this year.

"hashtag hot girl summer, Period." I scream with an renewed joy, ambitious tone, and just a splash of bad girl.

CHAPTER 1

Gazing into his eyes as if the world would come to an end any moment now she leaned in and asked "Have you ever loved someone so much that your world means nothing without them?"

"Is that a rhetorical question," he asks.

"No, answer the question I'm trying to be sentimental and you're being impudent."

"I can't say I have but I always wanted to feel that way towards a person," he replies.

Remember who you're loyal to because you wouldn't be anything if I didn't love you. The words of a lost love still echoing in my brain. Puzzled with thoughts of anxiety and stress, who am I loyal to? Would I be the person I am today if it wasn't for my lost lover who strayed away? So many unanswered questions flood my brain like a broken dam flooding a river over it's banks. Was I over compensating in love to the point where he no longer appreciated me? Did I come up short in compassion for his feelings? I can't wrap my thoughts around what went wrong, when, where, or how. I am left in a trance of unending anguish, lost in memories of him, searching for a door to open my heart again. Like a reptile in the swamp cold blood fills my veins, waiting for the day when he can bring warmth to my body again.

"I'm sorry you must be confused that happens to me a lot I drift off in my train of thought. Careless and free wondering what should, would, and could be. You are such a great listener though; for some reason it happens to me even more when I'm with you."

"Yeah at least one of us is listening, I wish I could get someone to listen to me for once" Joey says.

"Don't say that Joey I listen to you, see I'm listening now."

"I'm only joking with you I enjoy hearing your voice, I could listen to you talk all day."

"Yeah I'm sure you say that now, wait until the game come on, you is going to be telling me to shut up woman."

"No I won't, I might just say be quiet."

"Ha-ha they both mean the same thing one is just a little more polite," I respond

Joey has the cutest light green eyes ever so easy to look into and get mesmerized, dark brown hair, so jealousy of the silk smooth texture. Not that tall for the average guy but much taller than me. He has a very manly look about himself; he almost looks mean and angry if he's not smiling, extremely cute big ears and strong built frame. He has the sexiest war wound above his right eye. He said it happened when he was in the marines during training. I think it happened in battle or at least that's what I like to think it sounds much sexier that way. I known Joey since college but we never dated, we just grew to be great friends and he's a fantastic listener. He's almost like my personal psychiatric therapist I use to think he was gay when he didn't try to have sex with me when we first met or maybe that was me being insecure like every guy who meets me has to want to have sex with me. I realized over time that he is a genuine friend with no hidden agendas, excect for me to love him as much as he loves me. Of course he never came out and said it but I can tell. how is it that I am so blessed to have a man of such statue to listen to me ramble on about another man who no longer loves me?

Do I even love me? I know Joey wants to love, but why? How could a man so amazing love a woman so broken? Love a woman with so many sorrows and unsolved dilemmas. He has to be an angel like my father always says, be kind to everyone because you never know when you in the presence of an angel.

"Do you have any plans tomorrow," Joey asks, as his voice rips through my current thought.

"Your doing that thing again" he says. "Your day dreaming or drifting whatever you want to call it."

"I am not, I was just thinking."

"So what were you thinking about?"

"If you really want to know I was wondering why are you my friend, why aren't you off with some groupies, why are my problems important to you? I'm pretty sure there are plenty of women who aren't as broken and hurt as me, who would love to take up your time and give you the booty."

"Ha-ha" Joey laughs as he tips his head back on the sofa stomping his feet and clapping his chest. I can see his muscles flex in his arms as he bangs against his swollen biceps, Lord help me retain myself. He looks at me with that green sparkle in his eyes and I want him to take me right here, right now. Too bad it probable won't happen and I can't come on to him that's what sluts do and anyway I just got out of a relationship. What is that saying about how much I value my seven year relationship broken up or not? Plus we are just friends and I really need to buy me a dildo I have no one to ease my mind any more.

"You are really funny you know that. Well if you really want to know," Joey says, "I pity you."

"Pity me, huh what do you mean?" I say with a confused and insulted look on my face

"You are gorgeous Anne Marie; I adore your passion for companionship. Your sweet gentle spirit brings peace to my soul. Your soothing soft voice keeps my attention. All your pains and sorrows provoke my heart to be your healer. You are life with out war, you is harvest with out labor. You are more than a woman but no less than an angel. You are a rose with out water and I want to replenish the love dried up inside of you. You refresh me Anne Marie so I want to refresh you," says Joey. With sincerity and care in his voice; love and trust in his eyes.

I am mesmerized by the green glaze in Joey's eyes and deep tone of his voice, I am speechless. Oh my wow I don't know what to say. Who am I to be accompanied by a man so worthy. Every breathe he takes is a breathe he takes from me. I want my life to be his happiness. I want his joy to be my pleasure. I want his love to be inside of me, deep inside of me wrapped around my heart. I wish for only one day that it was that easy. I wish that I could flick a switch from sorrow and happiness, pain and joy, life and slumber.

"Joey I'm getting sleepy you should go now," I say in a low tone of hesitation.

"Did I say something wrong" Joey uttered with despair on his face as if he was looking forward to spending the night as much as I wanted him to.

"No, no it's me Joey I just need time to clear my head and think alone," I say as if I was the only one in the room trying to convince myself that's what I wanted.

He stands tall and grabs me whole, my face buried in his upper biceps strong and comfortable, I didn't want him to leave. I feel his soft, plush, moist lips leave my forehead like a gentle father kissing is new born. Why couldn't he have aimed a little lower, the possibilities that would've inspired if he did.

"I'll see you tomorrow" he says in a sad deep tone.

I wanted to tell him to stay but my lips would not move my voice would not crack; I was stuck in abyss of silence, trapped by the chain hold of my past lover who I could not let go. As he walks out the door, the frame of his bold shoulders nearly scraps the doorway as if he were a giant in a small world. What am I doing I think to myself? Why am I letting him leave? He shuts the door behind him and I turn the lock slowly with uncertainty and regret. I turn off the light and sulk on the sofa laying in sudden darkness. A ray of moon light spills through the broken part of the blinds. I pull my jeans off and let them sit by my ankles wondering if Joey was still here, and wishing my lost love never left. I slide my hands under my panties and place my ring and middle finger inside of me, parched for air as Joey runs through my mind. At the same time my last lover keeps flashing in my thoughts ever so often. 'Annemarie,' I hear his voice calling my name. *Kevin* I moan out and I take another breathe as I am drowning in my own sea of lust. Why did you abandon me I think aloud?

As I stroke myself I feel my body erupting, thoughts of Kevin and Joey explode through my brain. Why I am so blessed to have one and why am I so cursed to have lost the other? I fall asleep deep in my pleasure, drifting, daydreaming or what ever you want to call it as Joey puts it. Taken back to a time when Kevin was mine.

Awaken by the laughter of Kevin's voice as he chats on the phone with his brother. Bunch of guy talk sports, cars, and women. Kevin was a very happy man who always looked on the bright side of things. He was joyful, high energy, full of life and himself. I love Kevin; he knows how to put a smile on my face even when I didn't feel like it. Kevin's the type of person who can light up your day with his laugh, so much life and hope in his laughter. I can't picture my life with out Kevin and I don't remember my life before him. I lay in the bed watching his every movement like it would be his last. His tall lean frame crooked up on the wall one size fourteen shoe crossed over the other. One hand draped by his knees as the other holds the phone to his ear. Rough black hair, chocolate complexion, I like to think of him as my double fudge dip of fun. Bright white smile with dimples on both sides, beautiful light brown eyes with long curly eye lashes. He was such a sight to look at; I gracefully make my way out of the bed and into the kitchen where he stands.

"Hey my baby dolls up let me call you later bro."

"Good morning sweetness," he says to me.

"Good morning handsome I see you are up early."

"Yeah I was thinking of hitting the gym before work."

"That sounds sexy I got a gym you could hit to," I seductively say

"Oh yeah lets go workout then," he replies with confidence

Kevin picks me up by the waist before I could speak again. His strong big hands firmly planted on my navel as he walks me to the bathroom, I feel like a little princess being carried away by her prince. I rest my head on his shoulders and a calm of peace settles over my body. The walk from the kitchen to the bathroom seems like a lifetime in his arms, I never want it to end. He sits me on the sink, he loves having sex in the mirror sometimes I don't know if it's me or himself that turns him on. He gently grabs my face and looks me in the eyes with out saying a word then kisses me ever so pleasant.

"I love Annemarie I will never leave you baby doll, you make my world complete," he says with truth in his eyes.

Then his lips go from talking to sucking my upper neck then my breast. I'm getting so wet and hot; I place my arms around him and hold on tight. He takes off every piece of clothing with such regard to my body. I feel so safe in his presents; I feel so free and needed with him. The way he touches me puts my hormones on edge to the point of insanity. I never knew love could feel this good, his body deep with in me every stroke of ecstasy melts my soul, cradled in his arms as his hips dance in my section of lust. I trust him with my mind, body and soul, trusting him with my life and well being; trusting him with my pains and pleasures. I release myself on his shaft shaken with joy.

"Oh Kevin I'm forever yours I love you."

CHAPTER 2

[A larming buzzing) Another dream about Kevin but it felt so real why couldn't it have been. My life really, really kind of sucks with out him. I always thought of myself as the pretty defense attorney with sexy bad boy criminal clients. Who paid me in cash and dick, I had it all planned out I would tell them they could get off if they paid me and slept with me. Why would they say no, don't they know I'm the sexy defense lawyer of their dreams? I would have been the greatest defense attorney ever and the most satisfied as well. Instead I'm alone, broken hearted and stuck at a minimum wage job at the mall. This boring life I live was way more exciting with Kevin in it. I remember when getting ready for work meant sex on the kitchen table or bathroom sink or living room sofa or bedroom dresser and Kevin's smile to lift my day before it started. Now getting ready for work means W.T.F. shoot me in head why don't you.

I was never this head strung over one man, I used to have a life with a lot of friends and guys who wanted to date me, who didn't care if I had a man. When I met Kevin he was so handsome and so jealous, it made me love him even more. I never met a guy who wanted me all to himself and refused to share me. I wanted to be his forever, his jealously turned me on so much I use to say and do things just to provoke the jealousness inside him. Then I would always make up for it with tantalizing pleasure. His captivating body was my canvas of euphoria. I would dispense my drawings of gratification all over him then hang them up in my memories of fame.

I walk out the door and got into my half fix, nearly broken, piece of shit mobile. I never realized how much my world sucked until Kevin left me and I don't remember my world ever being good with out him. I work at a clothing store in the mall, a very small mall in a very small town called Worcester, Ma. It's not the kind of small city where everyone knows each other but it's the kind of small town where it's hard to get lost. While at work this sexy guy comes in my store. He looks around but doesn't buy anything, why would he this is a women's clothing store, unless he's got a girl which I wouldn't' doubt given the circumstances. He should though, what woman wouldn't try to trap him. He probably got like four baby mamas and seven mistresses. Oh shoot he's walking to the register, okay look pretty girl it's about time you get over Kevin and he looks like the right man to do it.

"How you doing today gorgeous," he speaks softly looking me dead in the eye.

Yup he definitely got like six baby mama's cause he's too confident but it goes so good with his looks.

"Hi" I say in my shy voice, lord knows there is nothing shy about me.

"What are you doing when you get off work I want to take you out to eat," he says as if he knew me my whole life and I wasn't a complete stranger.

This guy didn't even ask for my name he just skipped over that part of the introduction like I'm wearing a name tag or something.

"I'm not doing much after work and I would love to go out to eat but I'm not sure if it would be with you."

"Relax Betty Boo I'm not trying to jump in bed with you just yet that comes a little later if you be a good girl or bad girl. I just want to enjoy your company you're cute."

Wow did this guy really insult me and compliment me in the same sentence? 'Betty Boo' who does this guy think I am.

"What is your name?" I ask him in a demanding tone like I'm the police.

"Nathan, what might your name be angel, precious, gorgeous, princess, just guessing."

"Ha-ha no my name is Annemarie and what do you do for a living player, prostitute yourself."

"Damn why so beautiful but so mean, girls like you are freaks in the bed though."

No he didn't just call me out like that. He swears he knows what he's talking about. I see I'm going to have my hands full with this one.

"Umm excuse me Sir Nathan I'm not a freak in anyone's bed expect my own."

"I bet, well that's good to know so let me get your number and I'll text my number to you and when you get off we can meet up some where for dinner."

I guess I should give him my number, lets see what Mr. Smooth Operator is working with. "Well since you tried really hard; and you are kind of cute why not."

"Kind of, oh wow that's a new one," he replies.

"Don't get cocky you didn't get the booty just yet, being cocky comes after you experience heaven on earth," I can't believe that just came out my mouth.

"Okay I like the way you think you just might be someone when you grow up."

"Ha-ha-ha for your information I been somebody, the questions is can you handle this somebody," what am I saying my hormones are completely taking over this conversation.

"I can handle more than you can dish out baby; call me when you get off."

I so look forward to it. "Okay maybe I don't know if I'll have time bye now Nathan."

I just got off work and I feel amazing. I actually got a date with sex a symbol, let me text him first.

Me: [Where are we meeting?]

Him: [Elites on Washington Ave]

Me: [Okay.]

I get in to my not so bad but still embarrassing for first date car. I arrive at Elites and valet get my car which was so not cool but that was the only parking with in a half a mile and I wasn't walking a half a mile. I am accompanied to my seat; he is there on time waiting for me. He stands up in blue jeans with gators on, leather jacket, white v-neck shirt, and gold cross around his neck and a diamond Louie V wrist watch. Okay now I'm impressed for real because I'm ready to jump on him right now.

"What's up baby?" He says to me.

"Hi you look nice," I reply

"You are the gorgeous one, pretty lady," he replies with sex in his eyes.

We sit down at the table; he might have some potential I know he probable takes a lot of girls here though.

"So you never told me what you do for a living," I ask.

"I make music; you should come to one of my shows sometime."

"Really you are a paid rapper or a hobby rapper because I never heard of you."

"This music industry is crazy they want you to have your own fan base and money before they give you money and fan base. I'm straight though I got everything I need to be successful."

"So you're are aspiring to be paid rapper?"

"Ha that's funny and what's your side job? late night comedy."

"It's just a question you don't have to get all in your chest about it Mr. Rapper Man, what do you do for fun."

"When I'm not having fun at work I like to spend my time enjoying beautiful women like you."

"Okay here we go again; Mr. Smooth Operator is back, well say goodbye Mr. Rapper Man."

"Are you implying that I am bi-polar," he ask

"No it was just a joke I know your not bi-polar you just got ten different personalities which is far worst then being bi-polar with only two."

"Ha-ha yeah I was right you really do have a comedy show," he says

"So what do you do to ensure you enjoy yourself with all these beautiful women you meet?"

"Nothing special, I do what every lucky guy in my position would do, simply appreciate there beauty and that shouldn't be very hard."

"Look at this you just know every right thing to say. So tell me what you would do to me if you got the chance."

"Chance, well wouldn't you like to know, but sorry I stick to the N.B.A Code nothing but action."

This one here swears he's doing something, I'll just go a long with his little 'talk game' he calls himself doing. He is cute and looks like he knows exactly what to do to me. We continue talking and eating, the food here is great.

"You ready to get going." He asks.

"Yeah we can go," I say.

So we are standing outside waiting in the line to get our car from valet and I'm hoping he's not a gentleman and gets my car first, please for once be a selfish jerk please. He grabs my hands holds them up to his mouth and kisses both my hands.

"Let me take you home with me," he suddenly says.

"But my car," I say as if I actually cared about it.

"Don't worry about it I come here often, I'm cool with the owner just tell me your plate number and he won't tow it and I'll drop you off back here tomorrow."

It sounds so tempting but I don't even know this guy he could have aids or be a serial killer or be some kind of rapper/rapist/pervert. He knows the owner of this place he must be some what important or he could be bluffing me.

"I'm not sure."

"Come on stop being lame you in perfect hands."

"Okay fine I'll go with you but if anything happens to my car I'm going to kill you."

"Your car is fine I told you, what your plate number is so I can text it to the owner so he knows not to tow it."

"No let's go give it to him directly so I know he got it," I say to challenge his truth about knowing the owner."

"Okay that's fine," he says.

We go see the owner in the kitchen office I give him my plate number and can't believe I am really putting my trust in this guy he better have some good dick all this trust I'm putting in him. Valet brings his car, powder blue jaguar sitting on some twenty two inch rims. I'm Impressed when we get into the car everything looks neat and new but smells like weed and it's that loud pack to.

"Do you smoke," he asks me.

"Not really."

"So what does that mean because this Og Kush I got will put you on your ass?"

"That's nice," I'm not sure I want to be on my ass to night I prefer to be on my stomach.

"Come on, hit this one time you have to smoke after you eat, it's like smokers rule 101."

"Good thing I'm not a smoker huh." He lights the blunt anyway with out my permission and it smells so good. Ugh I miss smoking Kevin got me into smoking weed I used to hate it until Kevin introduced it to me. Sitting here in his car with weed circulating through my lungs reminds me when I use to ride with Kevin he loved to just ride and smoke he said it relaxes him.

Damn why does every guy I try to date just remind me of Kevin. The whole point of this was to get my mind off Kevin.

"Let me hit that blunt, puff-puff pass, buddy smokers rule 102."

Kevin did always say if you want to get rid of all the problems brewing in your brain smoke weed, ugh I'm thinking of him again.

"At ease little mama I got you let me do this," says Nathan.

He passes me the blunt, well theres no backing down now. I inhale a long pull hold it for a second and take another long pull. Exhale, oh this feels so good, I feel so good. Weed makes me so horny this guy better be ready for it, because I'm going to let him hit this hello kitty tonight. I haven't smoked since Kevin left and damn why did he leave I miss being high with him. Sex was the best when we were high. Like I remember this one time we've been smoking all night and pasted out and that morning we both woke up still high, started smoking again before we could even brush our teeth. Mornings breathe and all we didn't care his penis was so hard that morning I'll never forget it. I was lying on his chest massaging what was cum. My mind was no where near earth but my body was right where it needed to be. He sat up and sat me on his rock solid stick, I felt every inch of it. We stayed in that position until I busted on his battle field. When he felt me explode all over him he laid me on my back while still inside of me and made love to me while looking in my eyes. I will never forget the sex faces he made that day so passionate and sincere. I've must of organism twice that day. We went from sex to making love to hard core fucking then back to sex and topped off the morning with a shower together. I look over at Nathan and he is rolling another blunt while driving and the one in my hand is still going.

"Here do you want this, I can't finish this whole thing by myself."

"No you keep it,' he replies. "I'm going to just roll another one I like smoking to the head anyway."

"You like to smoke to the head so how you do that."

"Ha-ha you are so green, I'm just saying I like to smoke by myself."

"Well excuse me you asked me to smoke mister I said no at first."

"I'm not mad I got more than enough to go around. You got your own and I got my own."

"What ever I'm not the one with the diseases like you to good to smoke after me."

"You are reading way too much into it little mama this is what I always do, most people are happy they get to smoke by themselves but for some reason you are offended."

"Maybe your right I'm sorry," I say in my baby voice.

After twenty minutes of driving, smoking, and listen to his rap mix tape which I wasn't really paying attention to, we pull up to Cliff Sport Condos downtown. Ok this guy might be for real, there is a waiting list that even the President has to get on in order to get into these condos.

I never actually been in these condos I just heard stories about how beautiful they are. So we walk in to the corridor and there is a three story ceiling with beautiful crystal chandleries hanging from above. We get on the elevator and he pushes the eleventh floor. There are only twenty four floors so at least we are almost half way up. We get off the elevator and we walk down the hallway to another elevator, see through glass elevator It was gorgeous it had fresh flowers hanging on the walls of the inside of the elevator with a soft red cushioned benched to sit on. He had to use a special key card to open this elevator. We took it all the way to the twenty third floor the elevator opened up right into his living room.

"Wow this is beautiful," I say in shock of how beautiful it really is.

This is some place a princess would live not an unpaid rapper. Come to think of it he never told me how he makes his money; he must be doing something illegal.

"Thanks wait till you see the bedroom," he replies as if he knows I'm going to sleep with him to night

"A-ha-ha no not funny next, please do not think you are getting laid just because you got a nice condo on the 23rd floor Mr. Rapper Man Nathan."

"It's actually a presidential suite if you want to use proper terminology," he replies with a grin on his face

"What ever smart ass you still are not getting this ass."

I hope he doesn't take me serious because I so want to give him the ass and all of my body for that matter, I want him to take control of me tonight and do with me as he please. We sit down on the suede maroon love seat in front of his 10 foot by 20 foot screen window. Looking into the night at the city, the scenery is so pretty. He hands me a glass of wine.

"Wow so you're a gangster rapper with style, I like that."

"Who said I was a gangster?"

"I was just assuming you a rapper and all so I just figured you were selling dope and gang banging. I mean it's not bad I'm not judging you or anything."

"Relax, at ease little mama I got this,"

"I am relaxed what are you talking about you got what."

(Nathan Laughs) "You're funny girl you know that, I like the fact that you're so green its attractive."

I look at him with a puzzled confused blush and say, "Thanks I guess."

"So you never told me how you make your money if you don't mind me asking"

"I do mind and let's just leave it at that," he says in a serious tone.

"I don't want to be with you one day and cops lock us both up for something I know nothing about."

"You worry to much nothing like that will ever happen I got this little mama."

"Okay Nathan what ever you say."

We sit there enjoying the night, enjoying each other when Nathan pulls out a bag of white crystal powder.

"What is that," I ask him.

"This is what you call mollies, why do you want to go to molly world," he replies. "Where's that I never heard of it."

"Ha-ha its outer space some where."

"Really stop playing with me where it at," I say with curiosity

"It's the drugs effect it makes you feel free and lost out in space, mollies world," he says. I look at him with uncertainty as he looks at me with confidence.

"I think I'll pass this time and just stick to the weed and wine for now."

"That's cool," he says. He pulls out a bag of weed it smelt so loud and strong. He starts to roll it up in a Dutch Master.

"So where is you from," I ask him.

"I'm from Long Island, NY where you from"

"Well I'm from here unfortunately boring old Worcester. Why did you come to this place its so bland?"

"I came for a lot of reason but my number one reason was because it's wide open for the taking," he says with an evil smile on his face like Joker from Batman.

"So you're going to be the one to take it," I say to him in a sarcastic tone.

"Of course I am little mama I got this."

I really like when he says 'I got this' it's to cute he's so repetitive. I think I might really like this guy, he seems so cool, laid back, and mysterious sexy. He also got some class and knows how to treat a woman and I don't ever see myself getting bored with him. I deserve to be happy again I owe it to myself. He leans over to me and places his hand softly on my face and kisses me.

"You are a good girl and those are hard to find now a days, I don't want to contaminate you with my pollution," he says.

"No, no, and no, your'e not going to I want this to happen... I mean I think you're a nice guy."

"Listen if you still think I'm a nice guy tomorrow you can call me." He stands up and looks down on me with a smile.

"Come on let me give you a ride to your car."

Shoot just my luck the one guy I want to throw myself at doesn't want to catch me. We ride back to my car in silence expect for the text messages he kept receiving. He's probable going to drop me off and go pick up another girl. Why does she get to be the lucky one this is so not fair. Why does she get to be contaminated with good sex and pleasure? It's all my fault trying to play hard to get I should've been a lot more easy going. We arrive to my cold, lonely car, my pissed off to be embarrassed car. I jump out the car with out saying bye, he jumps out behind me.

"Little mama what's wrong."

Did he really just ask me that, he gets me all worked up and horny and drops me off to my cold ass car and ask me 'what's wrong.' I turn around and look at him with fire in my eyes and a sense of anger in my voice.

"My name is Annemarie not baby mama or mama little or what ever the hell you be saying, go call one of your groupies and leave me alone."

He walks up to me looking so confident and sexy with a stupid smirk on his face. He puts his hands on my shoulders and rubs my arms, looks me in the eyes and kisses me. "Your special and I want you to remain special that's why I didn't want to rush things with you."

"Stop making me like you more than I already do okay, you've been a great host and very respectful I was just expecting something a little different" I say to him as quickly as possible.

"Hey it's late and getting cold out here just get in the car and head home and I will call you tomorrow, Listen little mama I got this just be patient."

He walks off and sits in his car but doesn't pull off. I get in to the car and let it warm up before I pull off. When I drive off he drives off in the opposite direction. I walk through the door of my apartment dark and gloomy apartment of mine. I turn on the lamp and pour me some grey goose and cranberry. I sit at the kitchen table and Kevin runs through my mind like always. Why the hell can't I get rid of you Kevin? Why can't I stop loving you, what did you do to me that got me so sprung over you? As I sip on the goose I just began to feel so lonely and depressed why doesn't anyone love me anymore. I sipped myself to sleep and woke up with the cup in my hand.

CHAPTER 3

I looked at my cell phone it was 11:13am and I had a text message, wonder who it's from probable Nathan telling me how special I am and how he wants to sleep with his groupies but not me cause I'm just to damn special to have sex with. Oh wow its Joey I haven't heard from him since our last encounter.

Joey:[*Hey good morning beautiful I just been thinking about you lately and I want to see you*]

Aw Joey has always been so sweet and nice to me. I think I feel like hanging out with him today and it's my day off so why not.

Me:[*Hey that was sweet of you I'm off today so we can hang out today*]

Joey:[*Ok I'll pick you up in an hour I got a long day planned for us*]

What does he got in mind and an hour is definitely not enough time for me to be get ready, I'm still tipsy.

Me:[*How about I call you when I'm ready*] Joey:[*Ok cool*]

I stay sitting down at the table feeling out of place and lazy but happy because I got a date someone loves me. What should I wear and where do I start. After piling through my closet like looking for a needle in a hay stack I find what I want to wear. A pretty dark blue skin tight dress with one shoulder cut off. Okay now what shoes do I wear, how about them white crystal heels I got, with my fake white Marc Jacob bag, he wouldn't know its fake, would he? He would have to be really gay to know my Marc Jacob bag is not real; in that case maybe I should bring it to make sure I got me a straight one. He is kind of nicer than average guys. Now it's time to get in the shower and do my hair. After several hours of contemplating how I want to do my hair it's 4:05pm and I call Joey.

"Hello," Joey say's in a dragging deep tone.

"Hey its Annemarie do you still want to hang out."

"Yea I'll be on my way to get you I'll calls you when I pull up," he says with much more excitement

"Ok sounds fine talk to you later." I decide to have me quick shot of goose before Joey comes. I get in the car and he looks so cute.

"Dressed to impress you look handsome."

"Me, look at you princess I feel like I'm in a fairy tale maybe I should go back home and get my pumpkin carriage." He replies.

Oh my wow I can't believe he really said that weak ass line. Really princess, pumpkin carriage, I'm just going to ignore that one.

"So where are we headed," I ask him.

"Well I was going to take you to lunch but it's a little passed that so we're going to skip to dinner and then I got us a room at the Stardom Hotel. I booked us an hour session for the spa as well."

Oh wow okay he might got some balls he's taking the initiative to have sex with me to night I like that. We arrive at Elites and it feels so awkward but it's not like I can say hey Joey I just ate here yesterday with a rapper who introduced me to the owner. So I just put my best smile on and act like I'm impressed. We walk inside and the same host that brought me to my seat yesterday is here today just great.

"Hi I have reservations for two under Joey Watts."

"Yes right this way," replies the host while looking at me like I just was found guilty in a murder trail. I don't know what her problem is but she need a fix her face. "You went all out didn't you Joey."

"Oh its fine you're worth way more than all of this so this is the least I could do for you."

"Aw your making me blush, stop it," I say just to flatter him.

So we're sitting there enjoying dinner when the worst thing in the world just happened to me Nathan walks in with another girl on his arm. Why me why today, I look like such a whore I was just hear yesterday with him now today I'm with another guy. W.T.F it's alright for him to have another girl I expected him to be a player but he really thinks I'm a good girl and this image totally contradicts what he thinks of me. To make it even worst he waves and smiles at me and has the owner himself brings us out the best champagne on the house. This idiot Joey just thinks it's a good gesture and tries to play it like he got ties with the owner. Not knowing that I know why that bottle was really sent to us. I have no choice but to smile and act like I feel totally comfortable. Nathan leaves before us he gets his food to go doesn't even sip any of his drink. I know he's never going call me again so much for being special. The dinner was still nice because Joey was so clueless it just made me laugh inside.

While leaving Elites the Host looks at me with a huge smile like she happy I've been found guilty and she finally got some justice. She's probable sleeping with Nathan to and called him up here, was this a jealous slut or an unlikely coincidence. We head to Stardom Hotel hopefully the night doesn't end awkward. When we get there we head to the room to put down our things.

"This should be so fun I think my body is long over due for a nice spa treatment," I say.

"Yeah your body will be well taken care of," says Joey.

Then he does the unthinkable coming from him only because he's so passive. He grabs my arm from behind spins me around in his arms and kisses me with meaning and force. It got me so wet I forgot all about the spa I just wanted him to take me right there right now and he did. He scooped my feet off the floor had me cradled in his arms walked me all the way to the bed and laid me down. He pulled off my clothes with a sense of urgency. I looked into his beautiful green eyes and seen a whole different man. He looked like a raging lion waiting in the silence to attack his prey. I was meat for the slaughter and I loved every minute of it. A sense of calm fell over my body like dew in meadows, I felt so relaxed and released. Joey might be the one I never seen this side of him he just took it with no regard to my safety or well being. Oh my wow Joey turns me on so much. It reminds of the time Kevin snuck up on me one early morning while on my way to work. This is something I really could never forget only because I was half traumatized and half turned on. The night before me and Kevin got into a little argument about him not being more spontaneous when it comes to sex. He loves to have sex but just discreetly and I'm more of an anyplace anytime kind of person. So I get up that morning already frustrated because for one I hate to argue and for two I didn't get any penis the night before.

When I left the house I could've sworn on my life Kevin was sleep in his boxers under the covers I don't know how in the hell he got up and dressed so quickly. Anyways I'm getting in my car I'm letting it heat up all of a sudden a masked man runs up from behind opens my door and pulls me out the car. I was so shocked and stunned I couldn't even scream or move right away. He opens the back door and throws me in the back seat face first. Now I start screaming shit just got real for me and things start to get to out of hand I thought I was just going to get robbed but I'm about to be raped. I scream for Kevin over and over again but he never comes to my rescue. This man lifts up my skirt and ejects himself inside of me, thrusting and pounding my interior. He is way to big and strong to lift off me so I just lay there taking it. Why isn't anyone coming to help me why doesn't anyone see this mans legs hanging out the backset of my car and wondering what the hell is he doing? After I cum which felt so good and disgusting at the same time, he pulls out and nuts on my ass I think I throw up in my mouth my stomach started to turn I couldn't believe it. What would I tell Kevin? The man slightly gets up so I can turn on my back and see his face. He takes off the mask and I wanted to cry and laugh at the same time. I pushed Kevin off me and told him I hate him. He went back into the house with out a word. That fact that he didn't try to dispute what just happened turned me on even more. Kevin was the cocky type that thinks what ever he does is acceptable only because it was him who was doing it. I was so much more in love with Kevin on my ride to work I had the best day ever. I knew from that day forward that I wanted to spend the rest of my life with him and no man would ever be able to replace him. He was already perfect in my eyes I just wanted to find a flaw in him but when ever I tried to he exceeded expectations and proved himself impeccable.

"Hey baby girl do you still want to go down to the spa," ask Joey.

Completely lost in my memories of Kevin I look aimless into the wall and answer him unsurely

"I guess we still can but I feel like I just left the spa thanks to you."

Joey walks into the bathroom and starts running the water in the tub. Five minutes later he comes out the bathroom looks at me with a smile and says, "I want to live in this moment with you forever."

I look up at him with joy and pain in my eyes. Joy because he really might be the one for me and pain because that means I would have to let go

JAHZAEVION "J CLIP" MOSLEY

of Kevin. He picks me up and walks me in the bathroom and places me in the warm huge bathtub with jets going all around the tub.

"It feels so comfortable in here," I say to Joey

"Good," he replies and picks up a rag and soap and starts to wash my arms slowly with a sense of passion. He continues to wash my whole body the same way. After an amazing wipe down he takes off his boxers and joins me in the tub. While sitting behind me he wraps his arms around me starts kissing on the neck then my upper back and shoulders. He lifts me up then sits me back down on his cock. Hard turmoil deep with in my circumference, easing my mind with thoughts of pleasure while filling my body with purpose and pain.

We get out the tub and the spa is the last thing on our mind, we are the spa. We sit on the couch cuddle up in front of the fire place enjoying soft tones in the background.

"I really care about you Annemarie I want to be your provider and protector. We've been friends for over five years now and I never tried to come on to you because I wanted to give you time to heal and get over your ex-boyfriend because from our conversations you were really in love with him and still might be. I want to be your healer I adore your beauty and perspective on life. I'm ready to be your man; I'm ready to be your happiness."

"I don't know what to say, I mean I really like you to Joey I really do and I could see myself being your woman and being happy with you. Not now though I still got a lot on my plate and a lot to sort out in my head. I'm not going to lie to you Joey you been here for most of my break up with Kevin but he had a huge impact on my life It's not as easy as it sounds to get over him, but I'm trying for you I swear I'm trying."

"That's all I want baby girl, I know you are, thank you."

The night falls heavily upon us and takes us away in a deep slumber.

The sun shines brightly through the beautiful rose red curtains.

"Wake up my super hero," I say to Joey.

"Hey baby its morning already, man I really didn't want that night to end," he replies.

"Don't' worry we will have plenty more like it, if not better."

"I look forward to it."

He kisses me on the top of my head and holds me tight under his chin.

We get ready to get going and head out the door, on the ride home it's very silent but our feelings for each other are very loud. We hold hands the whole drive to my house.

"Thanks Joey I really enjoyed myself."

I'm glad you did call me later," replies Joey

Then he kisses me one last time before he leaves and I could've sworn it was the longest kiss ever or it might've just been me tripping. When he pulls his lips off my lips he looks at me with such joy in his face it made my heart smile that I could be someone's joy and happiness again. I walk in the house feeling brand new and revived. I look at the time and I got less than an hour to get to work, I arrive to work on time barely. I didn't really care because my night and morning have been going so good can't nothing ruin my day. My co-worker Stacy is working today she is so cool and the closet thing I have to a best friend if one ever existed. We been working together for two years now and we know pretty much everything about each other, all we do is talk at work.

"Hey best co-worker in the world," Stacy says I as walk into work.

"Hey girl, how are you doing? I missed you these past couple days," I reply

"I know right, like where have you been when I'm working you're off and when I'm off you're working."

"I think Susan did our schedules like that on purpose being a hater because her old ass at work with no one to talk to." Susan is our supervisor; she is a nice sweet lady when she wants to be.

(Stacy giggles) "You're so ugly, so tell me what I've been missing in your boring life."

"Girl let me tell you nothing has been boring about these past couple of days."

"Shut up and spill the beans," says Stacy.

"Ok the other day at work this super sexy guy name Nathan comes walking in here and ask to take me out after work."

"Shut up your being ugly stop lying."

"I'm serious Stacy like he was fine"

"What did he look like?"

"He was tall, dark, and handsome in a nut shell."

"Your ugly I'm not talking to you anymore."

"Ok he got dreads nice soft hair not that long though. He dresses like a millionaire and he treats me like a queen already. The flip side is he is a player but I'm going to change that I'm going to make him faithful to me and me only."

"So when do I get to meet him," Stacy inclines.

"Um hold on let me think maybe never."

"What, are you serious Anne why not?" Stacy says in displeasure.

"I just told you he is a player and I know he's already sleeping with other women and I don't want him sleeping with my best friend/co-worker that's not cool at all."

"Ok what ever keep your ugly secret lover friend to yourself. I thought we were like sisters and we could share anything even guys who are already players."

"You're such a slut Stacy O.M.G I hate your guts right now."

"Shut up ugly you know you love me."

"Maybe but I'm not telling you," I cheerfully say.

"What ever you don't have to I see it all over your face ugly."

Stacy and I chat up all day at work about Nathan and Joey and all my little episodes I went through. She is so cool and fun to talk to I can talk to her about anything and for hours. Work fly's by when we work the same shift making easy money. While at work I get a bouquet of flowers, chocolates and a card sent to me

"Look at you girl somebody really loves you," says Stacy.

"I wonder who it is from," I say

"Open the card ugly and read it."

"Okay, okay I am," I excitedly say anxious to see who sent me these.

"When I'm dreaming of you it's hard to be awakened
You are the only girl in my life I can't escape from
I want to feel your touch on my heart it is yours for the taken
I want to fill your memories with my entire love making
The love I have for you is a must
Coke bottle thighs curves swing like golf clubs
Roller coaster hips silk smooth skin
Butter milk cherry complexion
Viagra vibe because you give me an erection

More beautiful than beauty so your beauty is beautiful
Plush, wet, juicy lips one taste you leave me bent
Tipsy off your love no other could contend
You're the greatest woman that ever lived."
Love Joey

"oh my wow that was so cute Anne."

"Yeah but we not in love I don't love him," I quickly reply.

"Stop being ugly this guy is perfect for you, he is exactly what you need to get over Kevin. He is going to treat you good, be faithful to you and caring what more do you want out of a guy."

"I don't know I'm just not ready to commit to anyone just yet."

"Yeah right because if Kevin came walking in here and asked you to get back with him you would drop your heart on the floor and say 'hell yeah I love you Kevin I been waiting for you to come back'."

"Shut up I do not talk like that stop making that voice"

"Say it isn't so," Stacy replies.

"Probablyut who cares we both knows that's not going to happen."

The rest of work was kind of a drift for me. My mind was racing between Kevin and Joey I didn't know what to do. I think I need to create some space between me and Joey until I can get my thoughts together I don't want to rush in to this when I'm not even over Kevin. I leave work in a trance I don't know what to do about my love life. I get to the house and put the flowers Joey got me in some water. I sit at the table and start eating the chocolates I received. As I bite down into the piece of chocolate memories of Joey stroking inside of me arouses my hormones. All I want is his big bold shoulders on top of me while he reconstructs my intersection with his jack hammer. I pick up the phone and call Joey but no answer, I call again no answer. I've should've known he was just like every other guy hit it and quit it, but why did he send the flowers and write that heart felt poem. Something must be wrong let me text him, email him, face book him, twitter him, instagram him something. Ugh why do I feel like this? Fifth-teen minutes later my phone rings and it's Joey.

"Hey baby girl sorry I missed your calls I was in the shower."

Umm shower, the thought of warm water and soap dripping down his perfectly formed muscles almost made me drop the phone.

"It's ok; I just wanted to thank you for the flowers and poem you sent me today at work."

"Your welcome gorgeous," he replied "but is that the only reason you called me."

"No," I said in the softest baby voice ever.

"I'm on the way," said Joey as if he was reading my mind.

Then he hung up with out saying bye. I am so shocked with Joey lately he is really turning me on, doing things and saying things I would never expect from him. I don't know what promoted the change but I like it. The next morning I wake up to Joey's huge frame hovered over me.

"How did my beautiful angel sleep last night?"

"Perfect thanks to you baby," I reply with delight.

We kiss and don't stop; we kiss for God knows how long. I dig my fingers in his back and pull him closer if that was even possible. He enters me with such ease stroking time away, still kissing each other while he massages my middle with his rod. We stop kissing to catch breathes deep inhales we both take. He rolls me over on top of him grabbing my hips tightly as I belly dance on his pole. My right hand dug into his chest with my left hand crawling through my hair. Moans of lust fill the air; I can feel his body throbbing inside of me as his jolts my world. Electrifying pleasure static ran through my veins. He lifts me up off of him and sits me on his upper biceps. While squeezing my ass he starts to pull me closer to his mouth. I already know what's about to come and my pussy is soaking with anticipation. He puts the lower part of his face in my bosom. His chin hairs tickle my inner thighs. He eats me whole as I run my hands through his soft, smooth, dark brown silk hair. I grab the back of his head and pull him further inside of me. I look down and ask him, "can you breathe down there" in my out of breathe voice

He doesn't reply just continues to gobble me; if I didn't love Joey before I just might after today. We lay on the bed both exhausted and hot we look at each and smile. He grabs my hand and closes his eyes.

"Joey you know I have to go to work in a little bit."

"Yeah but I just want to enjoy you for a little while longer," he peacefully says

I look at the time and I have a couple of hours before I have to be at work. So I lay there with him and close my eyes. When I wake up I realize I'm two hours late for work.

"Wake up Joey I have to go I'm late for work I fell asleep I felt like I just closed my eyes for a second."

"Ok I'm up, I'm getting up baby," says Joey while yawning

I get dressed as quickly as possible and call in to let them know I'm on the way. Susan wasn't very happy to hear that I was late but she wasn't going to fire me.

Joey walks me to the car "goodbye baby girl have a good day at work."

"I will try I know I'm going to get written up for being so late but Susan will be okay it's not like our store be busy or something."

Joey kisses me one last time before I drive off and it was a wet one. After work I get in the car and charge my phone, it went dead on me. When I turn it back on I got a voicemail. I call it "What's up little mama call me I want to see you."

Why now Nathan I thought you were done with me and things are going so good with Joey I'm not going to call him. On the ride home I get another call it's from Nathan I don't pick up I want to pick up but I can't Joey has been so good to me. He calls back again I pick up this time.

"What do you want Nathan," I aggressively say

"At ease little mama, I got a show to night and I want to take you with me nothing else."

"I don't know Nathan me and that guy you seen at Elites are talking now."

"So is he your boyfriend."

"No not yet but he can be." I say with a puzzled look on my face

"Listen I just want to show you a good time no funny business."

"Ok what time is the show?"

"I'll pick up at 11pm."

"Okay fine see you then."

I get home and take a long hot bath; I shave and do my hair up real nice in a bun with two bangs hanging. I get a text from Joey:[Hey baby girl can I come over and spend the night with you]

Damn what am I going to tell him I already told Nathan he could pick me up and I'm really looking forward to seeing him again actually?

Me:[I told Stacy I would go over her place and comfort her she's having guy problems]

Joey:[Okay just call me tomorrow or something] [Okay]]

It is past 11pm and Nathan still has not showed up so I call him

"Where the hell you at Mr. on time for being late I didn't even want to go in the first place," I dramatically say

"At ease little mama I got this I'm outside."

"No your not I'm looking outside right now."

"I said I was outside not outside your house." (Nathan slightly laughs)

"What ever asshole it's not funny," I say trying to hold back laughter Come outside I'm turning on your street now."

He hangs up and I see his powder blue jaguar coming down the street it looks so sexy with the street lights glissading off the paint. I walk outside and he gets out the car and walks up to me.

"You look amazing and your butt looks juicy in them jeans."

"Stop and thank you lets go you already late."

"No I'm right on time come here and let me taste you."

I put my arms around his neck and he grabs my waist and we kiss like lovers who been away from each other for to long. We get in the car and head off.

"Where we headed," I ask him with a peculiar look on my face

"Relax we going to Club Shadow on 9th street is that alright with you, do you feel safe."

"It's alright with me I was just asking and no I don't feel safe but that's what's turning me on right now it feels dangerous."

"Ha-ha, you something else girl you're going to make a player turn his player card in one day."

"If that's even possible for you do you know how many hearts you would have to break in order to do that?"

"As long as it is not your heart I'm breaking."

"Sounds good," I look at him with my face knotted up.

We get to Club Shadow and its jam packed; there is a long line of girls outside waiting to get in. We pull up to the front door and Valet gets our car we walk through the front door past everybody I felt like a superstar. All them jealousy whores looking at me with there face cut up wishing they were in my shoes. Half of them girls probably already slept with him and they are looking at me like I'm the stupid one. Well I'll be stupid tonight bitches because I sure am enjoying myself while you wait in the line in the cold, getting patted down like your some type of criminal.

While sitting in V.I.P Nathan's buddies show up with a bunch of girls

26

and they all sit down and order bottles of Moet. Nathan rolls up and passes me the blunt, all the other girls that came with Nathan's buddies are licking that white stuff called mollies off thier hand. I ask one of the girls, "What does that do to you."

"It makes you feel so good inside and hyper you could ride that dick all night on a molly," the girl says

Sounds tempting I think to myself, I picture myself on top of Nathan for hours, orgasm after orgasm.

"Let me try it," she hands me some.

"Put it on your tongue and swallow," she says

I do and I feel normal at first later that night I don't' know if it was the Moet or weed or mollies but I feel so happy and loose. Nathan brings me on stage with him while he performs I can't see anything but bright lights but I'm having so much fun, everyone on stage is dancing and jumping around. After he performs we go back to V.I.P and some girl comes up to me and pours her drink on my shirt

"You stupid bitch what the hell are you doing with my man." The girl yells at me

"What the hell, O.M.G what are you talking about," I reply in shock

She continues to yell some nonsense I can't understand due to my intoxication. Nathan steps in front of me and tells his buddies to get her out of here. They drag her by her arms out of V.I.P. she is still yelling but can't anyone really hear her with the music so loud. We get ready to leave the club and on our way to the door a fight breaks out between four different girls. This one guy jumps in because I guess his girl was one of the girls getting her ass kicked. Nathan and his entire entourage surround me to make sure no one touches me. I felt really special at that moment. After bouncers break it up and send them outside we walk out the door. As soon we get in the car we see the same guy who jumped in the fight get shoot by the girl who he punched.

"Fuck, get me out of here Kevin." I was scared shitless I never seen a gun up close never mind someone get shoot.

"What did you call me, is that the guys name you were with at Elites."

"I'm sorry I'm just scared I'm not emotionally or morally equipped to handle all of this shit just get me out of here."

Nathan speeds off out the parking lot and down the street. He takes

JAHZAEVION "J CLIP" MOSLEY

me to his 'Presidential Suite' condo. I feel so horny and elevated I think the molly really kicked in.

"I took a molly at the club one of the girls gave it to me"

"Yeah you must be feeling wired up right about now then," Nathan replies

"Hell yeah, you know you look so sexy Mr. Rapper Man Superstar."

"You know you sound so drunk but still look so edible."

"Take control of me daddy do what you want to me I'm ready for you."

"I doubt it but we are going to find out."

He slams me up against the wall and rips my shirt off then lifts me two feet off the ground and starts sucking my breast. Then he gets down on one knee while kissing my belly; unbuttons my jeans and pulls them off. He puts one of my legs on his shoulders and slides me up the wall as he stands up. The leg that was dangling he holds up with his other arm. With my pussy right in his face and my head nearly touching the ceiling I spread my hands on the wall and let him take me. He licks me like a kitten thirsty for milk. I bust and he swallows it all and keeps stroking me with his tongue. Then he carries me to the huge cooking counter in the middle of the kitchen and lays me on it. My back is so cold from the contact of the marble tops. I arched my back up so I wouldn't feel the chill and he puts his foot on top of the counter and sticks his dick in me I thought it was all the way in then he pushed up closer to the counter and moved all the way inside of me it felt like his forearm was in me. It was so deep I tried to push him back out of me but he was to strong and I tried to crawl away but he was holding tightly on to my hips. I just took the pain as he clearly controlled the situation and believe me it was more pain than pleasure. After he pulled me up to his chest while still inside of me walked me to the couch, my head swinging like a rag doll as he carried me. He turned me around and bent me over the back of the couch. He felt even deeper from behind I can't even speak all I could do is moan and look out the ten by twenty foot screen window into the city. I wish I could fly right about now because I would fly out the window that's how deep and painful his cock is right now.

I don't remember when I went to sleep but when I woke up I was so swore. I feel like I've been raped last night I woke up on the floor in front of the bathroom door. I remember having sex but not this much sex. I got up and looked around for Nathan and he's no where to be found. I get my cell phone and call him.

"Where are you at, how are you just going to leave me like this?"

"Relax little mama about time you wake up. I had to make a run I'll be there in ten minutes I'm on the way."

"Bring me some breakfast since you want to be Mr. Out an about."

"Sure thing little mama I got you."

So I find my clothes all over the house and my shirt is ripped in half like what hell happened last night. I go through his closet to look for a shirt; I take a shower and I could barely stand my virginal is aching in pain I feel like I have a Comcast remote stuck up me. When I get out the shower and get dressed I sit down then I feel a sharp pain shoot from the middle of my chest to my virginal. Nathan walks through the door with some Starbucks.

"What did you do to me last night I feel like I was raped with a pool stick?"

"Close to it," he replies.

"I'm serious what happened last night."

"I can show you better than I could tell you."

He pulls out his dick and tells me to suck it and it wasn't even hard

"What are you doing I'm not sucking your dick I'm hungry and I want to go home."

He pulls my head back by my hair and looks at me with a scary smirk on his face

"You are going to do what I tell you to do now suck it."

There is no way I could over power him or get out of this situation so I put his soft penis in my mouth. He holds on to my hair and with both hands and strokes my face. His dick gets hard and huge I can't even stick half of it in my mouth, now I know why I am so swore. He looks down on me and pulls his dick out and lays me on my belly.

"No please don't, I'm so swore it hurts really bad."

"Bitch shut up you took it all last night."

"What's wrong Nathan what did I do to you? please stop this is rape."

He enters me anyway and it was extremely painful I started crying and he still didn't stop. I could barely breathe with him lying on top of me I started wheezing and my head was aching. I was crying for so long snot started running down my nose. He gets up and I look down at my virginal and it is bleeding, I'm balled up in a fetal position and kept crying.

"Since you got twenty one questions I got a question. Who the fuck is Kevin? You were calling me Kevin all night while we were fucking."

I look up at him and wipe my eyes and with a crack in my voice I tell him "I'm sorry can you please take me home please I just want to go home."

"Get your shit on lets go."

We get dressed and leave out, I get to the house and before I could get out the car he grabs my arm and looks me in the eyes and says, "I still want you, sorry if shit got out of hand just got a lot on my mind."

He lets me go I don't say a thing I just get out and walk in the house. It never felt so good to be back in my own house in my own bed.

"God please if there really is a God in heaven please help me. I'm calling on you Lord I need your help and guidance I need your direction. I just want a peace of mind, Lord please be kind to me. God have compassion for my situation I need your mercy and grace. (I start crying) God what do I do with my life; I put it in your hands God I do not know what to do, I just want peace and happiness Lord is that too much to ask please."

My phone starts ringing and I don't even bother to look who it is. I really need to decide what I'm going to do about my love life. I can't live like this going from guy to guy trying to fill a void.

"I fucking hate you Kevin for making me feel like this," I yell at the top of my lungs and start crying some more. I cry myself to sleep when I wake up I look to make me something to eat. How about a chicken salad with cranberries and almonds, that sounds tasty. My phone continues to beep with text messages. I look at my phone and I have six missed calls from Joey, Two missed calls from Stacy and text messages from Joey, Stacey and Nathan.

CHAPTER 4

I call Stacy "Hey ugly where you been," says Stacy. "You don't even want to know I had the best night and worst morning ever."

"Spill it girl tell me what happened."

After a couple hours of talking to Stacy I told her everything expects for the rape I left that part out. When she asked why I had the worst morning ever I told her because the night was over and I wanted it to last forever. I check my text messages from Nathan I have two.

[Call me when you get this] [I hope you still aren't mad about this morning I thought you would be into that kind of stuff]

I can't believe I fell for such a jerk. O.M.G what is wrong with you Annemarie. I call Joey hopefully I got one good guy left in my life.

"Hey baby girl I been calling you is everything okay," says Joey

"Yeah I just been really tired and wanted to rest in I'm really swore. Nothing serious it's just that time of the month for me and I'm cramping."

"Let me come over and take care of you baby girl," he says with concern in his voice

"Sure that would be nice."

"Okay I'm on the way see you in a bit," he hangs up

I got a serious head ache I hope he's up to taken care of me because I sure need it.

Joey arrives 15 minutes later I wasn't expecting him to get there so quickly. I let him in and he just grabs hold off me and swings me around in his arm at a slow gentle pace.

"Hey baby I missed you," says Joey then kisses me all over my face like a newborn.

"Hey I think I missed your company as well, but I have a really bad head ache I just need to lay down."

"Okay perfect I know just the cure." He scoops me off my feet once again like a precious rag doll and carries me into the bedroom. He places me on the bed and looks around the room.

"What are you looking for," I ask him

"Do you have any lotion any where?"

"Yeah it's in the bathroom cabinet." he walks off into the bathroom and comes back with the lotion.

"Lay back and just enjoys and I promise you won't have a head ache when I'm done."

He pours lotion on his hands and starts massaging my hand; he has very soft firm hands to look so manly and what ever he is doing is relaxing and it's working I don't even fell my head ache anymore. He continues to massage my forearms and shoulders, and then he gets intimate with it and moves to my breast and waist line. If this did not feel so good I would tell him to stop. Down my thighs to my calves then feet; he takes his time on my feet like each toe needed extra attention. This feels so relieving and soothing who would've thought a man could make my body feel so good with out orgasm. I fall asleep while Joey was still pleasuring my body. I wake up the next morning Joey is gone and my mind drifts back to Kevin, I wait all day for his call, I cant take it anymore so I call him."Kevin where you been I've been calling your phone all day."

"I been out with my friends and I didn't hear my phone."

"Why do you smell like soap and perfume, where were you at don't lie to me."

"I was out playing ball and I took a shower at my friend's house and his girl gave me a hug good bye and she had on perfume."

"You just got the perfect lie for everything don't you?"

"You really tripping and need to chill out I don't want to hear this shit."

"Let me see your phone," he passes me his phone.

"Why is your call log erased, what the hell Kevin I know you been with some girls."

"look stop tripping who do I come home to everyday, you right so that's all you need to worry about when I stop showing up then you could worry."

"Don't try to sweet talk me Kevin that shit isn't going to work this time."

"Look I'm tired beautiful I just want to lay down and enjoy your company can I do that please just for a little bit then you can nag me later."

"Whatever I'll leave you alone but I know you been messing with them girls out there don't expect to get no booty from me until you get checked, I'm not catching sexual transmitted disease's because you can't keep your dick in your pants."

"Are you fucking serious Anne, you really think I'm burning?"

"No I really think your cheating and them filthy sluts you sleeping with are burning."

Kevin walks into the bedroom and buries his face in one of the pillows.

"Don't you walk away from me I know you been sleeping around just tell me the truth I already know."

"If you already know then why are you asking me?" he looks at me with a serious stare.

"So you are cheating I knew it, how could you do this to me Kevin." I walk out the room and mope on the sofa with my knees to my chest arms wrapped around them and face between my thighs.

"You are so dramatic I said 'IF' key word being if."

"Leave me alone I don't want to talk to you," I reply

he comes sits down beside me and rubs my back I try to shrug him off as if I didn't want him to continue but I wanted to feel his touch and I'm glad he didn't stop even when I tried to make him.

"Look I love you and you only I'm not cheating on you I think you're just paranoid and you have no reason to be. You got a good man and you know it; you think these other women could take me away from you? Never in a million life times would ever I leave you."

He picks me up and carries me into the bedroom and lies beside me. His warm body is comforting heat to my soul. I feel protected and loved cradled under his heat. I fall into a deep relaxing sleep. All this damn time I been dreaming

I wake to Joey's arm draped over my breast and memories of Kevin flooding my skull. I push his arm off of me and sit up, he is passed out. I look for my cell phone to see what time it is and it is 10pm. I basically been sleep all day but I don't feel as swore as earlier but I still have a slight pain. I get up and walk through the house collecting my thoughts. I seriously miss

Kevin; I need to hear his voice right now but I have no way of contacting him because he changed his number and last I heard he moved to Boston or something. My phone rings and it's Nathan, like what is really up with this guy he is really starting to scare me and I'm about to get a restraining order out on his ass; fucking rapist. I need to call my dad but I really don't want to hear his gospel mumble jumble I just want some plain worldly advice. My father is a pastor and a very devoted Christian too bad I can't say the same about his only daughter. My mother passed away giving birth to me and my dad said I'm some kind of miracle gift baby from God, I don't remember how he put it. I grew up with so much pressure trying to please my dad and be a good Christian that when I got old enough to be own my own I never went to church or looked at a bible again. I had to go to church almost every day out of the week I went to church more than I went to school, like really who does that. I am so sick and tired of church and my dad can't seem to figure out why, really dude if you wasn't shoving that shit down my throat 24/7 maybe I might want to go to church on my own. I guess that's all preachers' kids, the parent preaching wants their kids to be extra holy as an example to other people in the congregation and all it does is back fire. I think if my dad knew what I was really doing out here with my life he would have a heart attack. That is why he will never know I love my dad and don't want him to die because I wanted to be reckless. He already lost my mother and never remarried; he still thinks his daughter is a virgin until marriage and that's the image I want to keep. I walk back in the room to see if Joey is still sleep, he doesn't look like he is getting up no time soon. My sweet Joey, thank you God in the mist of my heart break and tribulation you send me an angel. I put some clothes on and take a ride I don't know where I am headed I just need to get some fresh air and think. Kevin got me into doing this whenever he had a lot on his mind he would take a ride to no where and smoke, but I don't have any weed so I'll just have to make due with riding. I tour the city burning up half a tank of gas then I decide to go see my dad, I text Joey. [Hey I went to go see my dad be back in a bit if you leave call me]

I get to my pops house and ring the door bell he should be woke if not he better wake up his princess is here. He comes to the door in a white tank top and long johns with his bath robe over it. I jump in his arms as soon as he opens the door and start crying. I really didn't want to cry I don't like my dad seeing me vulnerable I just couldn't control myself something came over me.

He shuts the door behind me and holds me tight in his arm without saying a word. After several minutes of standing in place I release myself from his arms and wipe my tears. He goes in the kitchen and grabs me some napkins and a bottle of water.

"I love you Annemarie I know you don't tell me everything going on in your life and it's not all my business to know you is a grown woman now and I respect that. You are my daughter and will always be and as your father I just want to protect and see you smile. I know it's been extremely difficult on you growing up with out a mother and I'm a man I can't teach you how to be a woman the way your mother would've been able to. I tried my best and I just wanted you to be successful and have a chance to make your wrongs and rights in this world. I'm sorry if I went somewhere wrong along the way I really wish your mother was here, I miss her."

I never in my life heard my father talk like this especially about him wishing my mother was here. He always used to say God has a better plan for her in heaven. My father covers his eyes with his hand I could see tears crawl down his face I couldn't take it I never seen my father cry. A heavy burden of guilt fell upon me I felt responsible for him crying and I fell to my knees and started praying. I don't know what I was praying for my mind was so cluttered and my eyes so watery. My father kneeled beside me with his arm around my back. We stayed there in silence for the next few minutes.

"I'm sorry dad for making you cry and disappointing you," I sniffle and mumble as I talk.

"Don't be I'm just glad you are here and okay."

We sit back on the couch and he grabs his bible, I knew this was coming there was no way I was going to be able to avoid this.

"I know you always get restless when I talk to you about The Word but it will bring peace to your soul I promise I just want to read you one thing.

"Philippians 1:23-24 I am torn between the two: I desire to depart and be with Christ, which is better by far; but it is more necessary for you that I remain in the body. NIV"

He closes the bible and places it back on the coffee table; looks at me with teary eyes and we both lunge at each other squeezing each other for dear life. Neither one of us seen the other cry this much, it made us cry even more out of pity and empathy for one another.

Moments later I get up and go in the bathroom to wash my face while looking in the mirror I see a scared, broken hearted, lost little girl. I need to be brave I need to be strong for my daddy; he needs me as much as I need him.

I say goodbye to my father and head back home. When I get there Joey is still sleep it's 1am right now and I can't go back to sleep. I sit on the bed by Joey just looking at him and admiring his beauty. I honestly feel a lot better when he's around; I jump on top of him like a panther pouncing on its prey. He makes an unfamiliar grunt turns himself around with me still on top of him and looks at me with a half smile.

"Hey sleepy head get up I'm bored," I say to him.

He stretches and yawns then grabs me and rolls on top of me

"Let me use the bathroom and I'll be back," he says

He comes back in the room looking fully woke like he just took a line of coke or something.

"I just looked at my phone what did you do at your pops house."

I totally forgot I sent him that text and I wasn't expecting him to ask me that question, it caught me so off guard that it took me a minute to respond to him.

"Nothing I just haven't seen him in a long time I really miss him."

"I know how you feel I never meet my father I just heard stories about him from my relatives. From what they say he was a well respected and feared guy."

"Aw I'm sorry to hear that Joey, what happened to him."

"They say he was running guns from state to state and the F.B.I was on to him then he disappeared while my mother was pregnant with me."

When he told me that I started to look at him different and I started to love him more. I don't know if it was sympathy or the fact we got so much in common or the sex or my emotions I just don't know.

"It's ok though my mother is a very strong woman and raised me to the best of her abilities; I never got caught up in any illegal activities because I didn't want my mother to lose two people close to her heart."

I couldn't hold it in anymore I don't know what is wrong with me today I been very emotional. I buried my head in Joey's chest and started crying he wrapped his arms around me slowly in shock but didn't say a word.

"I'm sorry Joey I been very emotional today please forgive me."

"No reason to apologize I just didn't know my life story would touch your heart like that."

"I went through something similar I never meet... I never meet..."

I was trying to talk but tears kept coming out and I couldn't say a thing.

"Calm down baby girl I'm here now, what is wrong?"

"I never meet my mother and, and I don't know I just wish I have."

Joey didn't ask me what happened he just looked at me with the most beautiful teary green eyes in the world.

"My mother died giving birth to me and my father never really talked about my mom that much because it hurt him so much to even think about her never mind talk about her," I tearfully say.

"This was meant to be Annemarie when I meet you that day at the YMCA you were running on the treadmill so long you nearly passed out of dehydration. I asked you what was wrong and you told me about your recent argument with your boyfriend at the time and you were trying to run all your stress and memories away," we both slightly laugh.

"Yeah I remember that day I was so embarrassed."

"It was cute though when you told me that I was thinking to myself what guy would ever want to argue with such a pretty face. You are gorgeous and funny I don't want to spend my time with anyone but you."

"Yeah you say that now wait till I start driving you crazy like I drove Kevin crazy you will reconsider what you just said."

"Maybe, (chuckles) but no I wouldn't if anything I would drive you crazy right back."

We start laughing it feels good to laugh I really needed this. We joke all night and laugh and forget about our sorrows. The next morning I have to go to work and Joey makes my morning as exciting as when Kevin was there if not more. Now I'm ready to have a good day at work. I get to work and Stacy isn't working today I should've figured with hating ass old hag in the building. Work was normally slow as usual until Nathan came walking in. He walks up to me with one hand behind his back but you can tell he is carrying something. He gets to the register and pulls his arm from around his back and he has a teddy bear and a card.

"I don't want anything you have to offer Sir Nathan the rapist."

"You didn't even open the card just open it little mama."

"if you don't' leave I'm going to call the police and if you come to my job or home again I will get a restraining order out against you."

"Okay I'm leaving you got my number just call me when you get a chance."

He walks out the door but leaves the teddy bear and card on the counter. After twenty minutes of looking at what Nathan left for me I open the card. Inside are two tickets to see a comedy show at Fox Woods Casino Resort and a hotel key card for one of their presidential suites. Who does he think he is impressing; all the money in the world can't get me to go out with him. He didn't even apologize to me what a jerk. I put the card back in the envelope and give it to Susan and tell her some one left this for her. When she opened the card I never saw her smile so much in my life, well at least one of us is excited. After work I go have something to eat in the mall food court. When I sit down to eat some girl comes sits down opposite of me. She looks familiar but I don't know who she is.

"Excuse me do I know you," I ask her.

"Not officially I work in the foot locker we seen each other before but never talked or anything."

"Okay so is there something you want," I impatiently say

"Yeah I just want to be your friend you seem pretty cool and I could use a good friend in my life right now."

I look at her puzzled like how do I respond to something like that.

"Well guess we could be friends what's your name," I ask.

"Amy and your Annemarie right."

"Yeah how did you know my name," I ask her with curiosity in my voice

"You have an admire lets just say."

Okay I don't need any more of them I say to myself.

"Can I call you sometimes so we can hang out have slumber party or something."

"Sure," I say with no thought that I will ever contact her.

We exchange numbers and she skips away like a little kid in a candy store.

I don't know what that was all about but this has been a very interesting day so far.

I get done eating and I'm on my way out the door when a guy starts walking beside me trying to get my number. I usually tell them I got a boyfriend and

I'm faithful and that is enough but this one here was very persistence and it was cute. He walks me all the way to my car trying to get my number.

"What's your name," I ask him

"David," "well if I see you again David then maybe."

I get in my car and drive off he stands there with his hands in the air like what happened.

I wanted to give him my number he looked like he would be fun but I got enough men in my life right now. I get to the house and I'm beat I had a long day I take a shower and go right to sleep.

"Baby doll look at this house online it's huge I talked to the realtor and they only want a 5,000 dollar deposit that's not bad for a house this big."

"Baby come look, are you ignoring me," Kevin says with aggravation in his voice

"Okay I don't know what is your problem, I am just trying to show you this house I thought we were supposed to be moving but you acting like you don't care."

"Okay since you don't want say anything and act like I'm not talking to you then forget you I'm out of here I can't deal with your stuck up attitudes anymore." He gets up and walks.

"Kevin what are you talking about I'm tired I just got off work got damn."

"Oh now you can talk, man you're full of shit Anne."

"Kevin why are you tripping I been working doubles all this week so we could have extra money to move of course I care."

"I don't know what you been doing all week you say been working double you could've been off with some other dude."

"Kevin I love you I would never do that to you."

"Whatever I been hearing shit about you around the city, you already know I damn near know everybody in the city."

"Of course I do so why would I do anything and I know you could easily find out. What did you hear about me and from whom?"

"You think I'm stupid, you think I'm too cocky to think you would ever cheat on me."

"Kevin you are really tripping right now, you are the one that be cheating not me."

"So if you really think I'm cheating then why the hell you are still with me."

"Because I love you Kevin and I can't be without you."

"What ever save that shit for another guy I don't want to hear it, just remember who you loyal to because you wouldn't be anything if I didn't love you."

"Kevin where you going come back, Kevin what the fuck," I yell.

He walks out the door and slams it behind him. That's the last time I ever seen or heard from Kevin.

I wake up with tears in my eyes I can't keep doing this I need some kind of closure. I search on the internet 'private investigator' on my phone and several websites and numbers come up. I call one and ask them to look for a guy named Kevin Michaels. They want 150 dollars a day for their search. Is there was a flat rate I could just pay because what if it takes you forever to find him. They said 10,000 dollars is there flat rate per person. Well in that case I'm better off trying to find him myself, never mind I tell them and hang up. So much for that plan to find Kevin, I guess I won't be getting any closure.

I get dressed and call Stacy and tell her I'm coming over. On my way to Stacy house my mind was filled with so many unanswered questions and I just needed Stacy to help me solve this crisis in my brain. I am driving faster than normal because I really just want to get to her house. I am crossing over Providence Avenue when I hit this guy speeding down the street on his motorcycle. He hits the driver's side of my hood and goes flying over my car. I slam the breaks and my head cracks the front window with tremendous force, I pass out. I wake up in the hospital with my dad, Joey and Stacy there.

I can barely see but I can hear them.

"Heavenly father thank you Jesus, heal my daughter Lord I'm begging of God please." That's obviously my dad.

"OMG girl you better wake up you look ugly when you sleep and I need my best friend back."

"Baby girl wake up, hey I see her eyes opening a little," Joey says with excitement in his voice.

"Lord thank you, hey angel how you feeling," my father says.

"Wake up ugly I know you hear me don't drift off on us," yells Stacy

"I'm up how long have I been out," I say in a low slow drag.

"You been out for three days," says my father.

"You're okay now," says Joey

"I wouldn't be so sure about that I feel horrible," I reply

"Just get some rest angel it's good to see you up again the doctor said he didn't know how long you would be in a coma," replies my father.

"What happen to the guy I hit is he okay," I asked

"Don't worry about him right now just get some rest," says Joey

I close my eyes and fall back into an easy sleep.

"Wake up baby doll I'm here, wake up your lover is back."

"Is that you Kevin, is it really you," I say with excitement and joy.

"yeah it's me I missed you so much I don't know why I left in the first place I'm so sorry for leaving you baby doll I will never leave you again I was a fool back then who took you for granted."

"It's okay Kevin I'm just glad your back I missed you to baby," I reply.

He kisses me gently and soft, I missed those lips more than anything, my double fudge dip of fun.

"What happen are you okay," Kevin ask

"I don't remember much I just know this guy on a motorcycle came out of no where and my head went into the window. That's the last thing I remember."

"I'm here now I won't let nothing like that happen again from now on I'm driving because we both know your driving sucks anyway."

"Don't make me laugh it hurts to laugh I got a serious migraine."

"Just get some rest baby doll I'll be right here when you wake up," says Kevin

"I don't want to I'm afraid if I wake back up you won't be here I've been dreaming about you every night and I don't want this to be a dream."

"It's not a dream feel my face I'm the real thing and I'm not going any where."

"Do you promise," I reply

"Listen I'm always going to be here gets some rest I don't like seeing you like this you need to hurry up and heal up so I can take you home and give you that real sexual healing."

"You're still full of yourself but I love it," I smile at him.

"Good night baby," he kisses me one last time and I fall back to sleep shortly after. I didn't want to go back to sleep I tried to stay up and look at him in the chair as long as possible but the medicine I'm on has me very sleeping.

When I wake up I look around the room but I don't see Kevin, where did he go. I hit the button for the nurse and she comes in shortly after. My nerves are working me why did Kevin leave he said he would never leave me again.

"Yes how can I help you," the nurse says

"I was looking for Kevin Michaels he came to visit me but he's gone do you know what time he left."

"Hold on one moment let me go check you visitor's log."

she walks back out the room, I must've been sleep for a long time for Kevin to have left he probably just went to go get something to eat he'll be back. The nurse comes walking back in the room with an uncharacteristic look on her face.

"I'm sorry no one by that name came to visit you."

"That's impossible he was just here we talked and he kissed me so I know it was real."

"I'm sorry ma'am you only had three visitors come see you since you been here and it's been the same three people no one new came to see."

"He probably didn't sign in," I reply with hope in my voice

"That wouldn't be possible he wouldn't be able to get by our security with out signing in first and showing his identification."

"I couldn't have been dreaming it was too real I know that wasn't a dream," I say in a troubled voice.

"It most likely was the medicine we have you on is very strong and some side affects are illusion, I'm sorry ma'am."

I break down and start crying with my face in my hands. The nurse comes over and checks my hear rate and ask "what's wrong, this Kevin Michaels must be important."

"No, he's only the love of my life that I can't get over."

"I had I love like that once," she replies

"What happened how you got over him?"

"I didn't I put a gun to his head and made him marry me now he's my husband of fifteen years."

"Oh my wow did you really," I stop crying in shock of what I just heard.

"Yes I did he said that was the sexiest thing he ever saw me do in his life."

"Well I would have to find Kevin first in order to do that."

"Don't worry, he will find you first now get some rest dear so you can heal up."

The nurse leaves the room smiling at me and I felt a little better but still disappointed it was all a dream. I close my eyes and doze off again.

I wake up to my father and two detectives in my room. I hope this is a dream what are the police doing in my room I hope nothing bad happened.

"Hey angel the police want to ask you a few questions about the accident just answer them truthfully," my father says.

"Okay no problem can I have some water first to clear my throat," I reply

"Yeah I'll pour you some," my father hands me a glass of water.

"How you doing this is Detective Combs and I am Detective Frost."

"On the night of the accident how fast would you say you were going," Detective Combs asks?

"I was going the speed limit why do you ask," I say

"Because forensic report show based on the impact you were going faster than the speed limit and so was he," says Detective Frost

"So why are you asking me these questions if you already know the answer."

"So you are admitting you were speeding," Detective Combs inclines.

"No I wasn't speeding I just told you, why are you badgering me."

"A man died as a result of the accident we are just following proper procedures," replies Detective Frost

"Are you serious he died," I can barely breathe I start wheezing and huffing my heart rate goes up and the monitor starts beeping. The nurse runs in and clears everyone out the way.

"She's having a panic attack everyone leave the room," yells the nurse

I wake up several hours later and the nurse is standing by me checking the monitor

"When will I be able to leave the hospital," I ask her.

"I'm not sure you have a lot of swelling around the brain and we need to watch it and make sure it goes down because if it doesn't you can get brain damage."

"How long do you estimate please just guess for me," I implore

"Usually something like this takes three to six weeks some people heal quicker than others some people heal slower."

"Thank you nurse," I say with despair in my voice

"Your welcome dear don't worry everything will work it's self out."

"I sure hope so," I say with lack of confidence

I'm sitting in the room watching television I can't go back to sleep when Joey comes walking in.

"Hey baby girl I missed you, I had to work sorry I couldn't be here everyday," say Joey with a smile

"It's okay Joey thanks for everything you done for me I really appreciate you."

"It's nothing I'm just glad to see you up, usually when I come visit you're knocked out."

"Police came to visit me and said I killed the guy on the motorcycle why didn't you tell me Joey."

"I didn't want you to worry you already had enough on your plate," he replies.

"Well I did worry Joey I had a fucking panic attack when I found out," I shout.

"I'm sorry I didn't want to stress you," Joey replies.

"Save your apologies I don't want to hear it."

Joey walks to the window and looks out the blind starring aimlessly.

"I'm sorry Joey I didn't mean it I'm just really tense right now."

"I know you didn't I understand you going through a lot."

"I feel so bad Joey I can't believe that guy died and it's my fault," I reply in misery.

"No it is not your fault don't say that Annemarie I will not let you take the blame for that."

"You probable right I just feel so horrible Joey what am I going to do."

"Just get some rest baby girl," he replies.

"No I don't want any rest everybody is telling me to get rest I'm tired of being tired I want to get the hell out of here," I yell.

Joey walks out the room with out saying a word and that probably was the smartest thing he could've done because I was pissed and ready to take it out on anyone. I'm flicking through channels but I can't find anything interesting to watch. Several hours of watching nothing the nurse comes in with my food and a card in on my trey. I open the card and it's a poem from Joey.

When I think of you my mind goes crazy
It takes me to a place we both enjoyed before
It takes me to your bedroom
Where we both are laying down enjoying each others company
Then I put my strong firm hands upon your soft smooth belly

LOYAL AFFECTION

I began to rub around your stomach
Then I sit up and look into your eyes
Your soul draws me closer to your face
Our lips make contact
Suddenly, just, slow, pure, amazing
Was our first kiss
Soft, wet, juicy, kind, outstanding
Was the feeling of your lips
While we are in our momentary kiss
I lay my body in between your legs
And press my hard abs against whom
I feel the heat rising from your lips
I feel the tension build in your hands
The love spreads through your legs
You're sweet, gentle, smooth, assertive, and passionate
Precious hands pull my shirt off my back
You began to pull me closer and closer to your body
To the point where there is no space between us
I apply my lips to your cherry, tasteful, kissable, delicious neck
I struck your vocal cords and you began to moan out my name Joey
I continue to please you then I let up
You stop moaning then just look at me
I bite my bottom lip and take a trip down south
I put my wet, firm, woman pleaser tongue in your body
Then a quick shout like a burst your energy
Comes from the depth of your whom to the tip of your tongue
You began to feel
Lost, pleased, taken, fulfilled, whole, loved, sexy, beautiful, devious, and wet,
Then there is a pause and I stick my
Hard, painful, enjoyable, baby maker inside of you
Slow, gentle, ease, it goes in you
Shouts, screams, moans, pains, feelings,
All began to shoot from your mouth
Wait, hold up, stop, please, no, aw, it hurts
I let up momentary and say
Baby if you feel like u want me to stop I will

You say no but…
Then I put my body back in yours before you could finish
You grip my back with your nails
Bite my shoulder with your teeth
I whisper in your ear and say baby I'm all yours
Then I lick the words write out of your ears with my tongue
100, 110, 140 is the temperature in the room we are in
Wax begins to melt candles began to burn
Our souls began to trade as we make love in every way
We lay back down on the bed
Exhausted, used, hot, sticky, drawn, sensitive, empty, and full of love
We look into each others eyes and we see our selves inside each other
Love, passion, trust, care, sacrifice, is what we have
Love, passion, trust, care, sacrifice, is what we share
After our long, extravaganza, dirty, sexual, barbaric, grand slam, night
We both depart from each other
No, stay, please, don't go, I need you, is what you say to me
So I look into your bright, sinful, gorgeous, innocent, tearful eyes
I tell you that I will stay with you for a little while longer
We are sitting on the bed holding each other in our arms
Proud, grateful, rejoiced, happy, excited, I am to have you in my arms
Then I started to feel sleepy so I rest my self in your arms
I don't know how long I was sleep but when I woke up
I was at my house in my bed hugged up on my pillow.
Come home soon baby girl I can't make love to my pillow forever
Love Joey

Wow Joey really out did himself on this one, I feel so bad for the way I talked to him earlier. He is nothing but sweet to me he really might be the one, let me call him and apologize and thank him this poem it really did lift up my day.

"Hello," Joey answers

"Hey baby thank you so much for the poem I loved it you are so talented Joey you really should write your own poem book," I cheerfully say.

"Thank you and I don't think I'm that good though." he replies

"You are Joey don't be modest I loved it so much you put a smile on my face and heart I feel so much better."

"I'm glad that's all I want is for you to be happy."

"Aw you're so sweet Joey I feel so bad for snapping on you earlier I'm sorry do you forgive me baby."

Of course you know I do I never held it against you," he says

"Thank you Joey talks to you later."

"Okay goodbye Annemarie."

I can actually go to sleep now I feel at ease as Nathan would put it. I doze off thinking about how wonderful Joey is to me. A couple weeks later I feel much better and the doctor said I will be leaving soon in a few days. I was so excited my father, Joey and Stacy where all there to share in my joy.

CHAPTER 5

Then the same two detectives who came last time came again, this time they didn't ask me any questions they hand cuffed my leg to the bed railing.

"What is going on here," my father yelled with anger and bass in his voice.

"She is under investigation for the murder for of Zack Tucker," one detective says.

"This is preposterous my daughter never murdered anybody," my father replies with rage

"Sir, calm down we have a key eye witness that says your daughter did not stop at the stop sign," Detective Combs says

"If she had he wouldn't be dead and she wouldn't be in the hospital under investigation," Detective Frost adds.

"Who, where are they let me talk to them," Joey demands

"That won't be possible you won't see the witness until trial."

"This is bullshit, she didn't kill anybody," Joey yells with frustration

"Sir, if you do not calm down we will have to take you in for disorderly conduct," the detectives replies.

"Calm down Joey it's ok," I say to him

"No it's not okay you got rapist, drug dealers, and real murders out there and you are spending your time trying to lock her up. Fuck you crooked ass police this is bullshit I wont let you take her you got to kill me first," Joey implies with fury in his voice.

Joey is raging over there his whole face red with tears dripping down his face. The detectives pull out there guns and tell Joey to get on the ground.

"Sir, face down on the ground," one detective says with his gun pointed at Joeys head

"Sir, get the fuck down or we will shoot," the other detective yells

"Fuck you come on man I wont let you take her," Joey replies

Now Joey is a big guy and looks even bigger and scarier when he's mad. The detectives had no choice but to pull out there guns I wouldn't go near him either if I was them.

"Come on now son think of Annemarie she doesn't need to see this," my father says to Joey in a soft tone.

Joey looks at me with tears in his eyes and says "I can't live with out I will die before I let them take you."

Joey rushes at the police officers like a raging bull and they put two in his chest.

Stacy starts screaming my father starts praying and I pass out. When I wake up my father is sitting in the chair beside me.

"Dad what happened to Joey?" I ask.

"Doctors said he's in critical condition one of the bullets is close to his heart," my dad replies

I start crying and compassion so deep falls over my body like rain in the forest. I am in love with Joey and now I know it.

"Daddy please ask God the heal him, please daddy ask God to save him," I ask my father with tears in my eyes

My father couldn't take seeing me so hurt and in pain he breaks down on one knee and starts praying and crying at the same time. I cry so long I get a migraine and I fall back to sleep. The next morning the doctor said I can be released and the detectives are there to take me in. I never had been in a police car never mind a jail. I was scared out my mind I didn't know what to expect.

"Don't worry angel I will get you out of there shortly," my father says

I get down to the station and as soon as I get in there I feel dirty, people in there look like the bums from 4th street. A lady officer put me in a room and tells me to strip I felt so violated, she makes me bend over and crouch. Then she puts gloves on and sticks her index finger inside of me it was the most degrading thing I ever experienced. After searching my clothes she lets me put them back on. They seat me in a cell with six other women I don't say anything I just put my hands on my knees and I look at the ground, I've been looking at the ground so long my neck starts hurting. A couple of other girls in the cell are chatting about how they got here and what they are going to do when they get out. One girl ask me, "what's your name white girl you been real quiet over there."

What was so ironic she was white herself, I don't know if she felt black because she's in jail.

"Yeah she has been real quiet hasn't she," another girl says

I don't say anything maybe if I ignore them they will just leave me alone

"So you deaf now white girl I know you hear me talking to you," the first girl says

The other girls in the cell start laughing and joking.

"Hey I think this is a rich little white bitch that got drunk at a party and is in here for public indecency."

The laughter continues I just continue to hang my head low and try to hold back the tears.

"Oh shit she's crying look at this bitch she is really crying," the white girl who thinks she's black says.

She pulls my hair and lifts my head I wipe my face in fear of what is to come next

"Please I'm sorry can you leave me alone please," I say while trying to hold back a river of tears

"Oh now the white girl can talk, what's your name white girl?"

"Annemarie," I say in distress

"Oh shit that's the girl that killed that guy on the motorcycle it was all on the news last week," another girl says.

"Yeah so you a killer, okay white girl," the first girl says then she lets go of my hair and leaves me alone.

After another hour or so they open the cell and call my name to get finger printed. I get finger printed and get my picture taken then they put me back in the cell. A couple of hours later they call me back out of the cell to see the nurse. She asks me a bunch of questions then she gives me a T.B shot and puts a blue seal around my wrist. I go back in the cell and they bring us a peanut butter sandwich, one vanilla wafer cookie and a small carton of orange juice. This is something they give to kids in daycare but my appetite was ruined anyway so I give my food away to the same girl who pulled my hair back.

"Thanks white girl but you are going to wish you ate this later when your stomach is aching, they don't feed us much in here," she says

"You're welcome," I reply

Another hour of listening to the girls chat about sex and men, the officer opens the cell and tells us to line up against the wall.

"Put your hands on the wall and spread your legs," the officer yells, "and keep your mouth shut."

They search us again all I can feel is a hand running over my body and up my legs over my virgina this is the second most degrading thing I ever experienced. After molesting us they hand cuff our legs and arms together, walk us down a corridor to the women's part of the jail. When we get to the cell block they un-cuff us and send us into the cell block. I walk in very slow and cautious the other girls are loose and hyper like they are used to this. Another officer hands us all a bin and tells us to stand on the wall. The officer assigns us all a cell and we go to them. I get in my cell and there is a huge fat black woman on the bottom bunk.

"Hey what's up it's about time I get a roommate it gets kind of lonely in here sometimes?" She says.

I put my bin on the top bunk with out saying a word and climb on top.

"So what's your name and what you in for."

"Annemarie," I say in a low tone trying not to offend her

"Oh that's a cool name my name is Jessica, I got caught writing fake checks. I got kids to feed so I had to do what I had to do."

"So what you in hear for selling drugs for your boyfriend or something," Jessica ask.

"No, I rather not talk about it I'm just in shock and I can't really think right now."

"Okay I know what you mean; this must be your first time in jail," she replies

"Yea it is," I reply with as much respect as possible

"That's how I was my first time I got picked up for shop lifting and I didn't talk to anyone come to find out more people were scared of me than I was of them."

Do you blame them I think to myself?

"You are big no offense but I was scared of you right away as soon as a saw you."

Jessica laughs and snorts after she laughs like Ms. Piggy from the Muppets.

"You don't have anything to be scared of I'm not going to hurt you, I'm harmless," she says.

"That's good to know so where are you from," I ask feeling much more comfortable talking to her.

"I'm from Boston but I just came out here to write some checks because everyone does it in Boston and it's a lot easier to get away with it in a smaller town so I thought," she replies

"So all your family is in Boston, do they know you are locked up?" I ask.

"They don't know I'm locked up yet but I wrote them a letter they will soon enough."

"I'm sorry to hear that," at least my dad knows I'm in here and at least I don't have any children I left behind she must feel terrible.

"Don't be I'm used to this it's just another day to me."

She sounds so calm I knew she has to miss her children I know I would. Maybe this is her way of not thinking of the pain. I wonder how old her kids are but let me not ask she probably doesn't want to talk about it.

"I hope I never get use to this," I say

"Yeah that's what we all say our first time but if you ever have a second time you have to be like that or it will drive you crazy."

"I guess so but I don't plan on having a second time," I reply

"I'm pretty sure you didn't plan on having a first time honey but you're here."

Our cell doors open and Jessica steps out.

"Hey come on it's free time we can play cards, board games or watch television."

"No thank you I think I'll just stay in the room," I feel a lot safer in here.

"Okay but you have to come out for count first then you can go back in."

I jumped down from the top bunk and step outside the room all the women are lined up against thier doors some women are dressed in jail uniform and some are in regular clothes like me. The officer walks around and checks everyones wrist to make sure they are who they are. After count I go back in the room and the door locks behind me I sit on the bed and stare at the bright light above me. Every second feels like a year, I wouldn't last a week in here. Jessica was right because I'm about to go crazy right now, this bed is hard as hell and I'm cold I just want to go home in my own bed. Right now I would settle for Nathan the rapist bed. I miss you Joey, I love you Joey, and I wish you was here with me.

"Hey baby girl," I hear Joeys voice ringing in my ears. I am finally over Kevin I don't care about him anymore all my love is for you Joey. I let my thoughts of Joey ease my pain of being in this predicament. Several hours later the door opens and Jessica comes back in and shuts the door behind her.

"You feeling alright up there," Jessica ask me.

"Yeah I'm ok just thinking about my future husband."

"Okay girl what's his name I want details," Jessica replies sarcastically

"His name is Joey and he is my super hero," I say with a smile

"Look at you girl getting goggly eyed over there as you talk about him."

"He is very special to me and dear to my heart I love him."

"I can tell," Jessica replies

"Annemarie Jackson, grab all your things and step out of the cell." a voice comes through the intercom in the room.

"I guess you getting out of here girl good luck with everything and go make love to your super hero," Jessica says

"How am I getting out what happened?" I say with a surprised but exciting look on my face

"Some one must've bonded you out girl you should be happy."

"I am happy I'm getting out but what is a 'bonded'."

"really girl, its when some pays money to get you out of jail like monopoly get out of jail free card expect this isn't free."

"Okay thanks for the chat Jessica and good luck to you as well."

"Bye girl," Jessica says as I walk out the room

The officer escorts me to the lobby where I was when I first came in and I get my phone and other belongings back and they let me go. My father is there waiting for me when I walk through the door. I run into his arms and feel so free like I was locked up my whole life.

"Hey angel have they been treating you good in there," my dad ask.

"I'm okay dad thank you for getting me out of there I was miserable in there."

"I know you were angel but you free now."

"So how did you get me out?"

"I had to put up my house but it's was worth it for my angel, I've would've put up my life to get you out." He says with a tear slowing coming down his face.

"Daddy I love you so much thank you."

Your welcome sweet heart," my father says while holding me tight in his arms

"Is Joey ok, how is he doing?" I ask.

"I'm not sure I haven't been by to check on him."

"Can we go now and check on him please daddy I love him," I say with puppy eyes

"Yes we can go and I can tell he really loves you after what he did, it was stupid but I know he really loves my daughter. Any man that would put his life on the line for my daughter has my blessings"

We both laugh and head out the door, now that I think about it, it was stupid but a sweet gesture and I love him for it. We get to the hospital and go to E.R where Joey is being held. When we get there he has tubes all over his body and looks peaceful sleep. My dear sweet super hero you put your self in this quandary for me. I walk over to Joey and kiss him on the forehead. The nurse walks in and I ask her, "Do you know how long he will be sedated."

"I'm not sure, the bullet is close to his heart but thanks to the muscle tissue in his chest it didn't reach his heart. The doctors are working around the clock to insure it doesn't reach his heart but they can't pull it out because they are afraid they might damage his heart because it is so close. Their best bet it to keep him sedated and let his body heal himself and push the bullet out further then they will be able to go get the bullet out."

"Thank you nurse," I reply

I kiss Joey one last time before we head out and my father takes me out to eat at Apple Bees. We used to come here a lot as a kid this is one of my dad's favorite places to eat.

"You and this Joey guy are serious," my father ask

"Not yet but we will be when he gets out the hospital."

"What does that mean?"

"We been friends for a while now and he's been hinting to me that's he wants to be my man, well he been doing a little more than hinting but basically he's been wanting to be with me for a while. After what he did at the hospital I know he is the one for me. I already been having thoughts that he was the one but I had to be sure now I am really sure."

"That's good to hear I'm glad you gave it sometime before you rushed into."

"Of course daddy you know your angel is going to make the right decision," I say.

"I'm proud of you Annemarie I really am, you put a smile on my face and bring joy to my heart."

"Aw I love you to daddy forever and always," I say with so much joy.

We lean across the table and hug each other. We leave Apple Bees and I drop my father off at his house he is letting me borrow his car until mines gets fixed he has an old truck he barely uses and he said he might as well put it to use. I get to the house and call Stacy right away.

"Hey girl what are you doing?" I ask her.

"Staying away from your crazy boyfriend, girl he ugly and I'm traumatized because of him," she says and has good reason to.

"You'll be ok boo come over and keep me company I don't want to spend the night alone."

"You ugly, what ever I'm on the way."

"Thanks boo see you when you get here," we hang up

Stacey comes over and we chat all night and don't get any sleep.

"What are you going to do about Kevin now," Stacy asks

"Nothing I'm over him I can care less about him," I reply.

"You ugly, you say that now but what if he came walking through the door you would jump all over him and you know it."

"I'm serious for real this time I am over him my heart is for Joey and Joey only."

"Yeah but that pussy is still Kevin's." we both laugh.

"Shut up you stupid and no it is not, this is Joey's pussy now."

"Umm hmm girl we are going to see," she replies

"What does that mean?" I ask.

"It means if or when Kevin pops up don't act you still got feelings for him."

"Trust me I wont I'm done with him."

"Good because I can use a little fudge chocolate in my life," Stacy says

"You better not, that's my ex."

"I'm only playing girl put your heart back in your chest I was just testing you, I knew you still had feelings for him."

"No I don't but that's still my ex and I don't want to see my supposed to be best friend with my ex now that's ugly."

"Yeah I know I'm only teasing with you ugly," she responds

We spend all night talking about boys, work, Joey, the trail and everything that just been happening lately. The next day Stacy goes home and I have to be at work. I get to work and it's a normal slow day as usual nothing exciting but I had enough excitement in my life for now. I got pretrial in three days and I'm not looking forward to it. My dad hired me a lawyer and the lawyer said because of the eye witness the prosecutor has I will do some prison time but hopefully he can get me a deal cut since I'm not a threat and have no priors. The deal would consist of me serving two years in prison, hopefully. Key word being 'hopefully' as Kevin would put it. I don't want to serve anytime not even three days I hated being in jail never mind prison. Time goes by so fast the next three days any other time it would go by slow. I get to pretrial my dad is with me and they read me my charges and ask me if I have anything to say my lawyer suggest that I don't say anything, so I don't. We leave pretrial my lawyer ensures me that he would probably be able to get me the bare minimum based on the fact I have no priors and a good driving record. Most people would be happy in my situation after killing a man with their car but I couldn't do anything but cry. The thought of doing twenty four months in prison got me stressed out. My case was all over the news the guy who died Zach Tucker played college basketball for Holy Cross University so he was well liked and well missed. I felt horrible, some people wanted me to suffer some people said it was just and accident and I shouldn't be punished I couldn't watch the news anymore it was making me cry even more when I heard the negative comments that were being said about me. I'm not a bad person but some people are making me seem like one.

CHAPTER 6

The next day I have to go to work but I call out because I was too scared to leave my house and to stress to get up and do anything. I really feel like dying, committing suicide doesn't sound too bad right now. While laying in my misery I get a knock on my door I figured it was a reporter or something so I didn't even bother to get up. Then I hear someone going through my window I get up quickly in fear and reach for my phone as I am about to dial 911 I see Kevin walking in my room. He stands there in the door way and doesn't say a word I sit on my bed looking at him without moving. I don't know if this is a dream or not but I hope it is. The last thing I need right now is Kevin coming back in my life confusing things. I am happy with Joey and that's how I want it to stay.

"What are you doing here?" I finally ask him after several minutes of just starring at each other.

He walks over to my bed and sits beside with he sexy smile he grabs my heart again and I hate him for it.

"I came to see you, you've been in a lot of mess since I been gone I been watching the news."

"Maybe if you didn't leave in the first place none of this would have happened to me. It's your entire fault Kevin."

"I know it is baby doll and I was wrong for running out on you. I just don't like arguing I'm a happy person and back then we were arguing a lot. You know I can't handle all of that frustration I didn't know what to do so I just left."

"Yeah you just left and never came back to me Kevin you left me to fend for myself so much happened to me and it's your fault Kevin I hate you," I say in anger.

He leans over and puts his arms around me and tries to kiss me

"Get off me Kevin I don't want to kiss you I don't want you to touch me just leave get out of my house the way you came in."

He stands up and looks down on me.

"Stop acting like a brat okay I haven t seen you in like for ever and I might not ever see you again if you get convicted for murder so suck it up. I'm sorry I left we both were going through a lot back then," he says.

"for some reason I am the only one who suffered out of all of this, I don't see you facing any prison time or go through what I went through," I reply

"I suffered you just don't know the half of it, do you think my life was perfect while I was gone well it wasn't," he shouts

"Yeah right Kevin your Mr. Happy all the time remembers you don't argue."

"You're really going to give me this shit now that's why I left in the first place."

"Well go head and leave then that seems to be your specialty."

"Don't penalize me I left out on you one time, one time in seven years Annemarie, so do not pull that shit with me."

"What takes place now Kevin? You just walk back in my life after eight months and expect everything to be all fine and dandy like it was before?"

"No but I do hope we can get back to that point, I still love you and I know you still love me, you don't just throw seven years down the drain. Come to think if it was all fine and dandy I wouldn't have left I want it to be better than last time"

"I didn't throw it away Kevin you did. Or do you have bad memory now."

"My memory is just fine I remember we were supposed to get married and have kids, I remember you telling me you will always love me, I remember me being your first and was supposed to be your last," he says trying to convince me to take him back.

"I remember you telling me you would never leave and you see how that worked out."

"Watch your mouth when you talk to me," he demands.

"Or what Kevin huh or what you going to do, hit me now, you left for eight months and came back a woman beater."

"Shut up I'm not going to hit you, you know I would never hit you."

"I thought you would never leave me either," I say

"I'm here now and I'm back for good," Kevin says in a soft tone

I look at him while holding back tears I want to tell him I'm in love with some one else but knowing Kevin he will convince me that I'm not and it's only been eight months and that I was cheating on him while we were together because how could I have fell in love so quickly. It's better off if I don't say anything right now. I going to have to tell him sometime I just don't know how, I wish he would've came back when Joey was over here then I wouldn't have to say anything. I don't know how I am going to get out of this situation can my life get any more complicated. Kevin sits behind me and starts rubbing on my shoulders I want to tell him to stop but a part of me doesn't so I don't say a thing I just shrug. He doest stop he pulls my back as I lay on his chest he rubs on my stomach and breast. Then he goes under my shirt and into my boy shorts and starts fingering me. I know what I am doing is wrong but it feels so right. I grab his arm to make him stop and end up sticking my hand down my boy shorts on tops of his. While he is kissing on my neck and massaging my breast with his other hand I bust on his fingers. Kevin knows he got me, know me and he takes full advantage of it. He grabs me by the thighs and pulls my legs up until I'm lying on my back and my head is between his legs. He hovers over top of me pulls down my boy shorts and starts pleasing me inside out with his tongue. I pull down his sweat pants and stick his jimmy down my throat. We stay in this position until Kevin gets up and turns me around facing him. He pierces my heart with every pump, we make the love I been used to my whole life and Joey is the last thing on my mind. I'm back in my comfort level, I feel like I can tackle any obstacle in my life with Kevin inside of me. We stay buried deep in emotions for the next few hours, we had a lot of making up to do. We go from the bed, to the floor, to the wall, to the door, to the hallway, to the bathroom, to the kitchen, and end up on the sofa.

"I love you so much you Kevin, you better not ever leave me again," I say to him with sex on my breathe

"I won't baby doll," he replies

"How did you know I would take you back what if I had a man?"

"Then his ass would be out the door because big papa's back dude."

I laugh to myself and he smiles at me that handsome smile of his, damn I hate that smile.

"What ever you're still cocky as ever, you haven't changed a bit."

"Serious what would you have done if some guy was in my bed with me when you came?"

"I don't know several things come to mind," he says

"Tell me I want to know," I say with excitement in my voice

"Well one of the things I would do is leave and wait for you to call me and apologize."

"What wait for me to apologize! you got some balls there mister because that might not happen."

"I know you Anne and that would be one of things I did."

"What ever, what else would you do because that plan sucks if you ask me?"

"Man shut up, (chuckles) another scenario that would happen is I get the hammer from under the sink and beat the shit out the guy."

"Ha-ha you crazy baby but that's sounds more like you," I reply

"I would also pull my dick out and be like when's my turn."

"Stop it Kevin now we both know you way to jealous to ever share me so don't play."

"Yeah you right I think I'll just stick to my second plan," he says

"What have you been doing these past eight months," I ask him

"To much and not enough If you know what I mean," he says while looking away in search for some answers

"No I don't know what you mean, why don't you elaborate for me."

"I went to Houston, TX my brother lives down there and you know my brother is a little off his rocker."

"Why did you go all the way to Houston in the first place," I ask with a curious look on my face

"Because I was madly in love with you and extremely mad at you at the same time so I wanted to be far away from you as possible so I wouldn't see your adorable face and think about getting back with you. That didn't work because I saw your face every time I closed my eyes and woke up wanting to be back with you every day."

"So why didn't you come back for me," I ask.

"My pride wouldn't let me I had to show you I was done and over you but in doing that I put myself through a bunch of unnecessary events."

"I know what you mean," I reply

"Ok let me finish my story," he says. "So I get to Houston and as soon as I get off the plane my brother comes get me and I get in the car, he's rambling on about how some guy stole something from him. I'm like how did any one steal something from your crazy ass, he said he let the guy borrow it but the guy doesn't give it back and we have to go get it back. I said, wait dude what do you mean we. He says, yeah me and you brother, you got my back don't you. I had your back when you wanted to escape your little love life. So I really had nothing to say because he is going to drag me along whether I like it or not. Then we get to Wal-Mart and I say what we doing here. He says the guy works here come on. I already know everything is about to go down hill for me, I should've stayed in Worcester is what I'm thinking. We go inside find the guy stacking food on the shelves and my brother ask him what did you do with my stuff where is it at. The guy replies, I lost it I already told you that over the phone. Then my brother points at me and says, you see him this will be the last person you see before you die. I'm thinking what the fuck really. We leave out the store and my brother is pissed because he knows the dude is lying so he pull up to this red station wagon and he says that's his car bust the windows out. I say in broad day light at Wal-Mart really. He said, yeah bust out the windows he stole from me he has to pay some way. So I get out and kick out all side windows and smash in the front window, get back in the car and he drives off with a smile on his face like he just did something. I knew from that day on it was going to be some bullshit while I was down there but I didn't want to come back to you because I didn't want to hear your nagging."

"Oh what ever Kevin my nagging is better than what your brother put you through,"

"Not really, anyway let me finish girl."

"I don't even want to hear any more," I say but I really want to hear it all

"Shut up just listen," Kevin says.

We get to his house and my leg is killing me I lift up my pants and I'm bleeding all down my leg with glass stuck in it. I jump in the shower and the all the glass does come out but some of it went deeper in my skin, see look."

He shows me his leg where the scars are, my poor baby let his brother get this handsome body marked up.

"Later that day we go to the club me my brother and his friend Mike. So we're at the club just having a good time, girls every where like always."

"Umm hmm I'm sure you loved it," I say.

"Anyway it was a typical night just having a good time when my brothers see a guy in there, you testified at his trial a few years back. My brother instantly goes from having a good time to wanting to kill him. I'm thinking how does someone just flip a switch like that but then again this is my crazy ass brother that we are talking about. So he grabs me and Mike and tells us we need to go outside but on our way out he stops and tells me to stay in here and make sure the guy doesn't go anywhere. Now it wasn't a very big club but its a descent size so I'm keeping an eye on him and he starts walking out the door I follow behind him. When we get outside my brother and Mike are there waiting for him. There are no bouncers at the door just a promoter and some girls collecting money. So there was no one there to save this guy from my brother. One of the girls goes and gets the owner and he comes out trying to calm my brother down. My brother says ok I'm not going to do anything and turns and looks at Mike and gives him a node. Mike swings at the guy repeatedly. I am behind him so I join in on the action we beat this guy up half way through the parking lot. Then Mike pulls out a gun and starts hitting the guy in the head with the gun, blood is everywhere some even squirts on me. after beating this guy out the parking lot Mike goes to shoot him but the gun doesn't go off I say let me see I try to fire it but it wouldn't go off it was jammed from when Mike was beating him with it. The guy gets up and runs off in the woods."

"Wow Kevin this is not the Kevin I know you tried to kill man what is wrong with you."

"I don't know I was just in this 'I don't care mood' after I left you," he replies

"I think you were in that mood before you left or you would not have left," I say.

"The very next day my even crazier cousin comes by and I haven't seen him in like ten years so he wants me to go out with him. I know he doesn't have a license and he always to carry a gun where ever he goes but how could I say no I haven't seen him in ten years. We are driving around the city and we stop at this apartment complex, now my cousin drives a 1971 Monte Carlo on twenty four inch rims. When we stop a bunch of people come up to the car saying hi, mostly girls, but they were all ugly so you don't have nothing to worry about."

"I'm sure I don't, you do not have to lie to me, just finish your story before you piss me off."

"Anyway we get out and we just hanging around when someone comes up to us and says, hey police coming into the apartment complex. We jump back into the car and drive deeper into the complex. We get out and run into one of his girl's house. The only thing I'm thinking is why the hell I didn't stay at my brother's house. I didn't come to Houston to get into any bullshit I just wanted to get away from you. The police clear out twenty minutes later and we head back out. As soon as we pull out the complex we see blue and red lights behind us. This cop came out of no where I was looking around and didn't see any cop cars before he hit the lights on us. I knew right away we were going on a police chase this is what my cousin lives for escaping the law. That's exactly what happened we went on a police chase. Swerving through traffic at eighty miles per hour we hit a pot hole and spin out. I'm stunned I can't even think never mind move, my cousin hops out and starts shooting at the police and runs off. Now I know I'm about to die police start shooting back at him and I get out the car and take off running in the opposite direction."

"Oh my wow Baby did you get away," I say with concern in my voice

"I'm about to tell you, I'm running through houses and woods and backyards I don't know where I am going I'm just running. I do not want to get shot by one of those raciest red neck cops and I don't want to spend my first time in Houston in jail.

"Thier not raciest just because you and your cousin want to break the law, they were just doing there job."

"Whose side are you on?"

"I'm on your side but don't just assume they are raciest."

"Oh now you don't want me to assume that's ironic because that's all you did when I was here."

"No I didn't I know you where cheating."

"How do you do got proof."

"What ever, I don't want to get into this, just finish."

"Now where was I before I was rudely interrupted?"

"What ever," I say just to piss him off

"Anyway I end up under someone's porch. There was hole on the side of the porch and I crawl in. then I call my brother and have him come pick me up. When I call my brother he starts laughing like it's all a joke I get even more pissed I tell me just hurry up and come get me. Just my luck it starts raining I'm getting soaked in the mud but I would rather be in the mud then shot or in jail. it takes my brother three hours to get to me, when he picks me up he tells me that it was rush hour and the rain made it worst. I really didn't care at that point I was just happy to be picked up."

"Wow baby them first two days were worst than my so called nagging."
He just looks at me turns his head and continues.

"While I'm down there I need some money to support myself, I fill out a couple applications but get no replies. my brother want me to be like him so bad that he's says hey if you want to stay with me you have to bring in some money knowing I been filling out five applications a day, he just wants me to commit home invasions with him."

"I hope you didn't Kevin I do not want to be in love with a criminal."

"I had to do what I had to do, but listen," Kevin replies.

"I tell my brother I will go with him this one time and hopefully that will hold me off until I'm able to get a job. We leave out 10am in broad day light; my brothers said that's the best time because no one is expecting to get robbed in broad day light. We get to this nice house in a sub division and we park in the drive way, get out and my brother walks up to the front door and kicks it in. I was not expecting him to do that I thought he was going to pick the lock or something. It was a loud bang when he kicked the door I was for certain we were going to jail that day but no one noticed. When we get inside he starts running around and looking for things to grab, he tells me to get anything valuable. I go up stairs and I find a bunch of jewelry upstairs I'm thinking Jackpot. My brother grabs a flat screen television, video games, and he finds some weed."

"You are not attractive right now Kevin I thought you were better than that, what if some one robbed us when we were gone. I don't want your karma coming back on us."

"Relax nothing is going to happen I know damn near everybody in Worcester if someone robs us I am going to find out."

"What is you going to do when you find out huh call your crazy brother and get it back."

"No I'm going to get it back myself now listen," Kevin demands

"We get away and get back to the house split all profits and we both end up with 7,500 dollars each after my brother sells everything."

"Where's that money now do you have anything to show for it."

"Girl stop, I had to support myself and pay bills," Kevin replies

"You telling your story like your excited you did everything you did."

"I'm not but I was happy when I got 7,500 dollars for doing nothing," Kevin says with a grin on his face

"You did do something Kevin you broke the law, ruined someone's family and took all thier hard earned goods."

"Maybe if you wasn't nagging me wouldn't have left in the first place."

"So just blame it on me, it's my fault that you decide to commit criminal acts with your brother."

"No but it's your fault I left therefore it's your fault for everything else that happened."

"If you want to play the blame game there is a lot I can blame on you to."

"What ever, just listen," he replies

"No forget you Kevin you don't know what I went through for you to come at me like that."

"Ok so what did you go through because I know it's no where near as bad as what I went through."

"You think you the only one who go through struggles Kevin get off your self."

"I didn't mean it like that baby doll come here I'm sorry honey boo-boo."

"Shut up," I say with a smile on my face as I walk over and cradle myself in his arms.

"My beautiful honey boo-boo baby," Kevin says as he holds me in his arms

"Okay stop saying that it was cute when you first said it now it just sounds gay."

We laugh, look each other in the eyes and lean in for a kiss.

"Man this one time we at my brothers house and my cousin come over he wants us to go handle this guy who broke into his car and stole his sound system, so we drive over to where the guy lives my cousin finds out who it was because the streets talk, you know."

"No I don't know but continue," I reply, feed up with all his criminal stories I feel like an accessory because he's even telling me these things.

"We get to the guy's house and my cousin kicks the door in then the guy goes to run out the back door. My cousin chases after him and slams his faces into the back window on the door before the guy can open it me and my brother go over to where there at and we all start stomping this guys head in blood is every where."

"Stop Kevin," I cut him off before he could finish.

"What's the matter baby I was just getting to the good part," he replies like he's proud of taken advantage of a man who was defenseless against three idiots.

"Please don't tell me about any more your criminal acts in Houston just leave them parts out."

"Okay baby doll," Kevin says as we walk in the kitchen get something to drink then go sit on the sofa.

"What did you do with all that money," I ask him

"I went shopping and went out to the strip clubs."

"So typical of you, you're such a guy."

"Last time I checked I do have a penis."

"That doesn't mean you have to think with it. Why didn't you get your own apartment or a car?"

"Because I was staying with my brother and he has three cars so I just drove his around."

"Don't you want your own Kevin something that you can say is yours and no one can take it away."

"I got you, that's my own and can't no one take you away."

Only if you knew is what I am thinking but it's not the right time to tell him just yet. I just kiss him on the check and smile at him.

"It was crazy in Houston but I loved every minute of it I had a lot of fun."

"I bet you did with all those big booty country cornbread women down there, we all know how much you like big butts," I say

"I like big butts and I can not lie. (Chuckles)"

"So how was Houston bad if you loved and had so much fun?"

"I mean it was high when it was high and it was low when it was low."

"Did you ever get a job down there or did you stop looking when you got that money."

"You know me best baby," he replied with a smile

"You make me sick Kevin I knew you weren't going to keep looking for a job when you told me you got that money."

"Listen though when my money started getting low I started looking for a job but wasn't successful."

"So what did you do, break the law again."

"No I went without I started eating less I was a lot bigger but I lost all the weight I gained because I couldn't afford to eat proper."

"Why didn't you just come back here, why did you put yourself through all that for no reason."

"Pride baby doll that's all I can say," he pitifully replies.

"Well you got too much pride, I love you and I would never let you go hungry even if you weren't my man."

"That's why I love you so much your'e so kind and sweet I wish you were always like that."

"I am always like this."

"No you are not because when you're not having a good day you get so ugly to me."

"What are you talking about?"

"You are beautiful Anne and your personality makes you more beautiful then what you already are. When you have a messed up attitude or you don't feel like smiling it affects your personality and takes away from your looks."

"So I have to be happy 24/7, no one is happy 24/7 Kevin not even you."

"I'm not saying that but can we go one whole month without arguing."

"I don't know I can't predict the future."

"Let me ask you this will, we argue at least once in the next thirty days?"

"Probably, no relationship is perfect Kevin."

"Yea but why can you predict that we argue in the next month but you can't predict that we wont argue in the next month. You don't find something wrong with that."

"People argue! damn what more do you want me to say?

"Why do we have to be like other people, why do we have to be a statistic?"

"We're not a stastistic, but we're not perfect either."

"That's not being perfect just because we go thirty days with out arguing I can see if we go our whole life."

"Maybe you should find some other girl you can be with that won't argue with you for thirty days because if I have a problem I'm going to let it be known. I'm not going to hold back my feelings sowe can go thirty days without arguing.

Is that what you want Kevin for me to be false and smile all the time when I'm not happy?"

"No I want to be genuinely happy all the time and smile because you want to smile, how I can make you that happy tell me baby doll and I will do it."

"I don't know how," I reply

"You never know is there anything you do know," he says

"Yeah I know we go thirty days with out arguing."

"So you want to argue with, you plan on arguing with me. Why can't you plan on not arguing with me?"

"Kevin enough with the mind fuck please I'm not trying to purposely argue with you I like being happy with you."

"That's what I'm saying I love it when you are happy it brings me so much joy and does so much for me when I see you happy. When you're happy my minds is clearer, my thoughts are more organized. My heart is lighter, my drive and ambition is high. I love feeling like that but I only feel like that when your happy baby doll."

"I like being happy with you too, but maybe we're not meant to be anymore," I say with insecurity

"Of course we are meant to be what you are talking about." Kevin replies as he looks at me with curiosity on his face.

"I mean maybe it's meant for us to go our separate ways now, I always thought we were meant to be until you left me then my eyes opened and I started see differently."

"So what, you were dating another guy while I was gone or something," he replies

"Not necessarily at least it didn't start off that way," I say

"What do you mean not necessarily it didn't start off that way? What happened when I was gone you slipped and fell on his dick or did he fall and land on your pussy."

"It was nothing like that he is my friend I known him for a while and he was here to comfort me when you were gone, I was heart broken and vulnerable."

"Spare me the sob story how did ya'll end up having sex is what I want to know."

"It just happened he was there for me when you should've been."

"So let me get this straight basically you were cheating on me."

"What," I say with a puzzled look on my face. "No I never cheated on you, what you are talking about."

"You pre-cheated," Kevin replies

"What does that even mean I pre-cheated how do you pre-cheat, you either cheat or you don't."

"You said he's been your friend for a while so while I was dating you this guy were in your ear telling you a bunch of bull shit so he could replace me that's why you were always arguing with me. You never argued with me that much in the first couple of years of our relationship but when this guy comes around you're so called 'friend' you argue with me damn near every day and drive me away so he could come in the picture and 'comfort' you," he aggressively says.

"No it's nothing like that we were just friends."

"Friends don't have sex Anne I don't go to the gym with my buddies then go thier house and have sex with them I don't even think of some shit like."

"Because there guys," I say

"That's not the point they are friends so they stay in the friend category they don't jump in the relationship category because me and you took a break."

"A break is what you're calling it, more like a break-up."

"What ever Anne, they still stay in the friend lane. So like I said you pre-cheated on me because if this guy wasn't you're so called 'friend' then you wouldn't have anyone filling your head with a bunch of bull shit and you wouldn't be arguing with me all the time. Therefore I would have never left because I would have been a lot happier."

"If your not happy now you can leave I don't care your going to leave anyway."

"See that's the shit I'm talking about just because you got feelings for this other punk you think you can just talk to me any ole way because you got a back-up. So if we don't work out you can always run to him. You think I'm stupid I already know what you're trying to do. You're trying to justify your self for cheating and now that you got feelings for this guy you're trying to make our relationship miserable so you can feel comfortable about leaving it and going with him."

I don't say anything I'm so pissed with his accusations I just want to rip my hair out.

"I love you Annemarie and I'm sorry for leaving you to fend for yourself and I love you to much to give you up to this punk whoever he is. You're mines and I plan on keeping you I'm going to fight for you what ever I have to do."

He walks over to me and cuffs me in his arms, we stand there in silence for the next few minutes until his phone rings he looks at it but doesn't pick it up. I know its one of his Houston sluts but I don't even bring it up. I go in the room and lay down Kevin stays in the living room watching television. What am I going to tells Joey, how am I going to tell Joey? He just took two bullets for me to prove his love; he's been there for me this whole time through everything. Now I got my ex/current boyfriend living with me, I can't kick him out because he has no where to go and I don't want him to go back to Houston that's not a good place for him. I just don't know what to do I got court coming up again next month, why is my life falling apart like this. I fall asleep deep in thought when I awake Kevin is asleep by my side. I get ready for work that morning with so much on my brain, Kevin, Joey, court, my future. I get to work and Stacy is not on shift with me and I don't really care, my mind is so cluttered I don't have any room for Stacy. The day is going by so slow, slower than normal it's probably because I want to hurry up and get off so I can go see Joey in the hospital.

CHAPTER 7

F inally the work day is over and I head to the hospital when I get there Joey's mom is in the room with him. I walk in and I see Joey's green eyes looking at me and he half smiles but don't speak.

"Hey how are you doing? You're Joey's mom right it's finally nice to meet you," I say. She looks at me with judgmental look and says, "hi nice to meet you I heard so many wonderful things about you from Joey."

"I sure hope so," I reply

"Joey just came out of his sedation doctor says he his healing fast thanks to his physical fitness."

"That's wonderful to hear I'm so happy."

"Doctor said he just needs a lot of rest and he should be just fine they took the last bullet out this morning," she says.

"Great that's good to hear," I reply not really knowing how to respond to Joey's mom.

What do I say sorry your son is so in love with me that he took two bullets for no reason to prove his love and now my ex-boyfriend is back and I might not even be with your son anymore.

"Can I talk to you for a minute outside right quick honey?" Joey's mom asks.

"Sure why not," I say knowing that this can't be good.

"Joey told me so many wonderful things about you he speaks highly of you every time your name comes out his mouth. He really adores you sometimes I get jealous."

"No you shouldn't you are the number one woman in his life," I say with a smile on my face

"The point I'm trying to get across is I never seen my boy so head over heels for any woman except me so you must be special."

"Thank you," I butt in and say

"He really must love to do something so stupid only love makes you do things so stupid. I just ask that you treat my Joey right and love him as much as he loves you if possible because I know that boy loves hard. He loves with his whole heart and he will sacrifice anything for you even his life as you already saw. Just don't break his heart it is very fragile he never had a father to raise him so he doesn't really have a tough side like most men, he has his mothers love in him and a lot of it. I don't want you to hurt my boy I don't know if I would be able to forgive you. He is all I got in this world he is the only reason I still want to live life so please take good care of my boy and I promise he will do the same for you. I know you are a wonderful woman and a great fit for my boy. From woman to woman I am glad it is you Joey loves so much if there is anything I can do for you just let me know you are family now."

If this isn't the best/worst news I ever heard I life. So much for perfect timing I got the best perfect timing for the worst times ever.

"Thank you so much, sorry I never caught your name?"

"Just call me Mama-T."

"Well thank you Mama-T I appreciate you very much and I am lucky to have a man like your son in my life."

"You're welcome dear anytime."

She holds her arms out for a hug and I walk into her space and we hug. She squeezes me tight like a mother would her child, like the mother I never had.

I walk back in the room and Joey's is coming in and out of conscience I give him a kiss on the cheek and tell him bye before my face comes raining down in tears.

I leave the hospital more confused and lost then when I got there, if I didn't know what to do before then I really don't know what to do now. I decide not to go straight home the last thing I need is Kevin clouding my judgment I call Stacy but she doest pick up she must be working 2nd shift. I call my new friend Amy she probable doesn't want to hear about my problems but I have no was else to talk to and maybe and outside perspective might be just what I need. Considering she doesn't know Joey or Kevin she can give me an honest unbiased answer.

"Hello Amy speaking."

"Hey Amy this is Annemarie from the mall do you remember me."

"Of course I do I've been waiting for your call I have you saved in my phone but I didn't even look at the screen, I'm watching my favorite show on television."

"I'm sorry is this a bad time?"

"No it's never a bad time what's going on," she replies

"I just need some one to talk to can we meet some where."

"Sure, how about we meet at Vick's Pizza on State St."

"That sounds perfect I'm not to far from there see you in a bit," I say

"Okay great I'm already dressed and I don't stay far so I should see you shortly."

"Okay see you then," I say and we both hang up.

I get to Vick's pizza before Amy and I have me something to drink while playing angry birds on my phone. Amy arrives shortly after me in a cute outfit she looks like she is about to audition for the bad girls club.

"Hey you look beautiful in that outfit," I say as she walks to the table to sit down

"Thank you and you always look beautiful no matter what you wear," she replies with a grin on her face

"So what's going on it's finally nice to meet up and hang out with you."

"I know I been caught up in so much drama lately," I say

"Yeah I know I been seeing you on the news."

"That's only the tip of the ice berg girl; I got two problems much bigger than that."

"Bigger than murder please tell," she says with an attentive look about her

"Excuse I have to use the bathroom first this drink ran right through me,"

"Sure what were you drinking I'll order us both another one."

"It was just a sprite."

"Ok two sprits coming right up."

I head to the bathroom, should I even be talking to her about my problems we just meet, I'm acting real desperate right now. She does work in the mall with me but that's not enough of an excuse to tell her my love life problems. I'm really tripping I just need to go home and have a nice hot bath that will help me clear my head. But I don't want to be rude I did drag her away from her favorite show the least I can do is small talk and have a couple drinks with her. I get back form the bathroom and Amy is sitting there with a smile on her face and two drinks on the table.

"Hey you alright you look at little blue," she asks me.

"I'm fine just a lot on my mind."

I pick up the sprite and have a sip and we small talk about where she and I are from but nothing to serious. A few minutes later I start to feel light headed and dizzy then I blank out. When I awake I find myself in what looks like a basement. It's dark with wood ceiling and cement walls. I am sitting down in a chair with my hands tied behind my back, directly across from me is someone else sitting in a chair with their hands tied behind them except they have a bag over there head. From the look of thier body structure it looks like a man, an elderly Caucasian man from the wrinkles on his skin.

"Is anybody out there, help me please? What's going on out there get me out of here," I yell. I see the door crack open and bright light rushes through.

"Who is out there," I scream with fear

The door continues to open and I can't see who is walking down because the light is so bright. I can only tremble with fear for what is about to happen to me. The craziest thoughts are running through my head I don't know what is about to happen I only expect the worst. I start to pray not that God saves me but that when I die he takes my soul to heaven.

"I know I been a horrible servant Jesus please forgive me for my sins and grant me repentance," I mumble.

The person walking down the steps get closer until I can see their shape it's a man he walks right up on me and says, "Hello Annemarie."

"Who are you what do you want from me."

"I want you to love me and appreciate me," the person says

The voice sounds so familiar, I can't pin point it in my brain, and that voice belongs to someone I know I heard that voice before. They walk over to the wall and turns on the light, I can't believe it, it's Nathan.

"What the hell is going on Nathan what are you doing to me, why am I here, how did I get here?"

"I told you before I still want you but you never answers my calls or return my texts so I figure if I help you then you would appreciate me and love me."

"You're sick Nathan how you are helping me by kidnapping me. Knowing you, you probably raped me while I passed out.

Nathan laughs and lights a cigarette. I start coughing as my lungs are filled with second hand smoke. He walks over to the other man tied up and pulls off the sack over his head. The man is badly beaten blood is covering his whole face.

"Oh my god what did you do to him Nathan, he needs to go to the hospital."

"This is John Wilson he is the key eye witness in your case the one who is going to try and put you away for murder."

"I didn't murder anyone it was an accident and my lawyer said I might be able to get two years, this man doesn't deserve to be beaten for that."

"You right Anne girl he deserves much worst he deserves to die."

"No he doesn't, do not kill this man over me or for me I will never forgive you Nathan,"

"Let me tell you something Anne I wasn't raised with a sliver spoon in my mouth like you I had to take everything I wanted in this world. I had to take my respect, my money, my women, and my love now I'm going to take you."

"Why Nathan who am I to you," I ask

"You are who I want and that's the only reason you need to know. I will tell you this I never knew my father and my mother left me in a crack house when I was three because she was a crack head and couldn't and didn't want to take care of me. Another crack head found me and took me in for a couple months then she didn't do anything after that. I still stayed with her but she didn't feed me or bath me. I remember being three years old eating anything off the floor I could find. When I was seven years old I ran away and a woman who looks similar to you saw me on the park swing one night and asked why I'm not at home I told her I had no home, she took me in and treated me good. She used to play with my penis and jack me off and suck it sometimes but I liked it. She showed me how to be a man and how to treat women. She died when I was fourteen of heart failure and her oldest son kicked me out the house. I was in the streets ever since taking what I wanted. When I see your face it reminds me of that woman who cared for me the only person that cared for me in my life. So when I found out this guy was trying to take you away from me I had to do something about it."

Nathan looks at me with an evil grin on his face pulls out chrome 357 rouge and shoots the elderly man in the head.

"Oh my god," I scream at the top of my lungs

"Help somebody help me," I continue screaming

"No one can hear you," Nathan says to me in a soft demonic tone.

"What are you going to do me please let me go I won't tell anyone."

"I know you won't tell anyone because you did it, while you were passed out I put the gun in your hand and fired it so your prints are on the gun not mine you see I have gloves on."

"What the hell Nathan no one will believe you, this is crazy."

"It's not what you know it's what you can prove a wise man told me one day. What I can prove is that you murdered John Wilson in cold blood so he won't testify at your trail. You have motive and it sounds very believable especially since your prints are on the gun."

"You will never get away with this Nathan I fucking hate you."

"Don't be so mean little mama I got this. Now you will love me and appreciate me or this gun will pop on the DA desk with your prints on it."

I start crying in shock of how my life is turning out and the fact a man was killed in front of me. I hear more foot steps walking down stairs it's a woman when I see her face I realize its Amy. She walks up to Nathan and tongue kisses him, I am so disgusted. She takes the gun from him

and places it in a plastic bag and takes it back up stairs with her. Nathan cuts me loose and I am too weak to do anything but look at him, I haven't eaten since this morning. He picks me up and carries me upstairs into the bathroom and warm water is running in the tub with bubbles. He sits me on the toilet and takes off my clothes then places me in the tub. I am aware of everything that is going on but I am too drained to do anything about it. He washes my body as the warm water and a bubble soothes me.

"I told you I still want you and I can never let you go Annemarie you are the one for me. I love you and I will have you even if I have to force you to love me. I got big plans for us, you, me and Amy will be one happy family. Now I won't force you to stay here but anytime you decide to go to the police or run I will make sure that gun pops up on the DA desk."

I don't say anything I just close my eyes but he knows I hear everything he is saying I just wish I didn't. After the relaxing body wash he carries me into a room and places me on the bed next to Amy. She is in her panties with no shirt or bra I am wrapped in towel. Nathan sits between us and kisses Amy and she starts taking his clothes off. He looks at me and says, "make love to me or I will beat you."

That fully gets my attention and I reply, "I am hungry Nathan feed me."

He snaps his finger at Amy and she walks out the room and comes back with a bowl of mixed fruit and some water. I eat and drink and regain enough energy to comply with Nathan's sick demands. I wake up with Amy's legs on top of mine I don't see Nathan but I hear him out in the living room talking on the phone. I can't really make out what he is saying but I know it has something to do with money. I kick Amy's leg off me and spit on her but she doesn't wake up. I get out the bed naked and walk in the living room where Nathan is, he quickly ends his call and holds me in his arms.

"I want to go home Nathan," I say

"Sure no problem, I'll give you a ride just remember what I said anytime I call you better coming running."

"I understand I just want to go home."

"I got you new dresses hanging up in the closet go put one on and I will take you home."

I head back in the room where Amy is sleep and get dressed, before I leave out I take one more look at Amy as she sleeps in peace and I smack the shit out of her with all my might across the face. She wakes up and looks at me but doesn't realize she's been smacked I smile at her and walk out the room. Nathan takes me home when I arrive he opens my door like the gentlemen he never could be and lets me out

"You have a good day little mama I will see you soon."

"Yes you will big daddy," I flatter him with evil intent

I walk in to my apartment to be greeted by Kevin asleep on the couch with his jacket on and cell phone in his hand. I'm not sure how am going to approach this situation I'm in but I know Kevin is going to be apart of it. He says he really loves me well we will see how deep his love goes for me. I take shower and rinse off all the nasty filth of Nathan and Amy, then I run me some bath water and bubbles and sit in and relax myself. Kevin comes walking in the bathroom while I'm in the tub with a surprised confused look on his face.

"Where were you last night I called everyone looking for you? Your dad is worried, I'm worried, Stacy is worried. What's going on what happened last night," Kevin asked

"I will tell you when I get out the tub just let me enjoy this warm water on my body," I say in a nonchalant voice like nothing is wrong.

"You're acting weird Anne and I don't like."

"Don't worry Kevin I'm going to tell you everything trust me, I want you to just give me a minute."

"Okay I'll be in the living room calling everybody letting them knows you are alright."

"Thanks," he turns to walk out, "hey Kevin," "yeah baby doll," he replies "I love you."

"I love you to girl I just don't like when you worry me like this."

"I know baby."

I get out the tub wrap my self in a towel and go in the living room where Kevin is.

"So what happened last night, tell me everything," Kevin says.

I tell Kevin detail for detail about how I meet Nathan and about when he first raped me. I tell him everything the happened last night and about Amy the only part I leave out is Joey. Kevin looks at me with fire in his eyes and pain in his heart as I am telling him every detail and the events that took place. When I am done and quiet Kevin bangs his fist on the glass coffee table and shatters it, his blood dripping from his hand and forearm.

I scream in shock, "What's wrong Kevin."

He doesn't say anything just gets up and walks out the door with a blood trail following him.

"Where are you going, what are you going to do," I yell as he shuts the door behind him.

I can't sit in the house by myself I am too paranoid I quickly get dressed and head to the hospital where Joey is. I sit in the room with Joey he is sleep but his presence even on a hospital bed is enough to make me feel safe. My phone starts to ring and it is the detective on the case.

"Yes what can I do for you," I say already knowing why he is calling

"I have a few questions to ask you can you come down to the station."

"What is this about?"

"It is regarding the case something came up and I need to talk to you at the station."

"Okay gives me a minute I'm at the hospital with the guy you shot but I'll be down there in a few," I hang up before he could reply.

I get up and Joey is sleeping peacefully I kiss him on the check and leave a note on the table next to him.

I'm in a tough predicament right now
I just want you to know if anything happens to me it wasn't your fault
And I love you, Anne

I head out and make my way to the police station downtown, I get there and both detectives on the case greet me at the door like they knew exactly when I was going to show up. They walk me into an integration room or at least it looks like one from the movies.

"Where were you Thursday night?"

"I was at home with my boyfriend Kevin."

"So that Joey guy is not your man."

"No he is just a good friend."

"He sure did take two bullets for you like he was getting some pussy."

"Do you have to be so disrespect officer?"

"I'm a detective first grade."

"Whatever, is that all you want I'm ready to go"

"No that is not all we want, why is the only person that can put you away in prison end up dead two blocks from your house."

I can't believe this stupid asshole dump the body by my house.

"I don't know officer I told you I was at home with my boyfriend, how did he die this is horrible."

"I'm pretty sure you know how he died," the other detective says

"Why would you think that I would never kill anyone?"

"Well you already got one under your belt that's more than most people, even if it was by so called accident."

"It was an accident and I didn't kill anyone I don't even know who the key witness is or was."

"We're going to check out your alibi if it checks out you're in the clear."

"So I can go now," I say in frustration.

"Sure but we're watching you."

I get up and walk out the building when I get in the car I call Kevin but no pick up. I call again and he picks up.

"Hey Kevin where are you detectives just questioned me and they will probably question you next."

"What did you tell the detectives," the voice of Nathan comes through the phone

"Who is this where is Kevin," I say with a nervous tone

"You still don't know my voice well don't worry will have plenty of time for you to get use to it after I kill your boyfriend with the same gun you killed John Wilson with."

"Fuck you Nathan where are you."

"I'm where ever you are how about you tell me where you are and I'll come pick you up."

"I'm not telling you."

"Then you must not love your man."

"I'm at the police station come get me."

"How about you drive home and I'll pick you up from there."

"What ever I'll call you when I get there," I hang up

I don't know what is about to happen or what am I about to do but I'm not even scared I'm just pissed. Nathan pushed my last button, its one thing to mess with me but when you mess with my man you crossed the line bitch. I speed all the way to the house when I walk inside Nathan has a gun to Kevin's head while he is on his knees. Kevin is beat up with blood all on my carpet.

"I see you already had an incident before I got here so I did not see a problem with adding to it, you need to get a new carpet anyway," Nathan says as I walk through the door.

I run over to Kevin and drop on one knee.

"Are you okay baby?"

"Baby, I thought I was your baby," says Nathan.

I don't pay Nathan any mind I continue attending to Kevin

"So you really love him don't you, well that's good for you because I have a perfect opportunity for you to prove your love." Nathan says

I look at him and turn away

"Suck my dick or I will shoot him in the head."

Kevin grunts and goes to swing at Nathan but misses.

"Don't do it Anne I would rather die then watch you suck his dick," says Kevin while spitting out blood

"I'm not going to let you die Kevin I couldn't live with out you," I say

"So what's it going to be Anne," Nathan says

"I crawl over to Nathan on my knees and unbuckle his belt. Kevin tries to get up but Nathan points the gun at my head and tells him not to move. I start sucking his penis for a few minutes I can hear Kevin in the background crying but he can barely talk because his teeth are punched in and his mouth is swollen. I can't take it I won't lay down and let Nathan control my life anymore. I bite down on his dick with all my might he screams and hits me across the head with the gun. I fall to the ground with my head bleeding. Kevin launches at him and tackles him the gun goes flying across the kitchen floor. I hurry up and grab the gun while Kevin and Nathan are wrestling on the floor. I pick the gun up and fire one shoot at the floor everybody stops moving. Kevin gets ups and grabs the gun out my hand and points it at Nathan.

"No Kevin don't shoot him please don't you are better than that just call the police."

"Kevin doesn't speak just grunts at Nathan and shoots him in the chest five times. I ball on the floor crying because I know Kevin is going away for murder and there is nothing I could do and this is the same gun used to kill John Wilson. Kevin puts the gun on the floor and wraps his arms around me. Twenty minutes later police show up I guess neighbors heard the shoots and called the police. They kick down the door with there guns pointed and handcuff both of us. Kevin manages to tell them I had nothing to do with it and they let me go. I go in the ambulance and Kevin goes in a different ambulance with the police. They stitch me up and I call me dad he drops what he is doing he comes over right away. He helps me clean the house and pull up the carpet. I don't know what I would do with out my dad. He doesn't ask me too many question but I know he wants to so I give him minor details with out telling too much. I don't want to give my dad a stroke. I stay the night at my fathers house only because he insist he said he would feel a lot better knowing I'm in the safety of his home if for only one night. So I cave in to his wishes anything for my daddy. The next morning the detectives show up at my father's house looking for me they take me downtown for questioning. When we get to the station they ask me questions about what happened last night I don't say anything because I don't know what Kevin told them and I don't want to go against what he said. After an hour of trying to get me to talk they tell me Kevin is going away for life I just sit there and wipe the tears that keep creeping out my eyes. They finally let me go and my dad is there waiting for me. My life is completely falling apart but at least Nathan's not in it any more. That is the only good thing that came out of all of this, then again I would've never gave Nathan the time of day if Kevin never left me so it was only right things played out the way they did. Oh what am I saying I'm never going to see Kevin again unless it's between thick pieces of glass with a telephone attached. I have to do something to get Kevin out of there but how. Amy, that's how that bitch is going to pay for this, I'm going to make her tell the police everything that happened or I'll be joining Kevin in prison. I rush over to Amy's house and she's not there I go to the mall and she's not there either. Where could this sneaky slut be at? I go back to the house and get some rest it's getting late and I been looking all over the city for this girl she probably skipped town or something. After I get out the shower I take some pain killers my cramps are killing me it's that time of the month already. I'm early probably because all this stress I'm putting myself through. I'm in the bed laying down when I get a call from the hospital it's Joey

"Hey baby you woke," I cheerfully say

"Yeah there letting me go my muscle tissue healed faster than expected I want you to come pick me up if that's alright I don't have my car"

"Of course baby I'm on my way you caught me just in time I was about to go to sleep I'm so glad you called me though."

"Thanks baby girl see you when you get here."

"Okay be there in a minute call you when I'm outside."

"Okay bye," we hang up.

I'm so excited my boo is coming home from the hospital I miss Joey so much I need him more than ever right now. I get to the hospital and I call Joey and he comes outside, I run up to him and throw myself in his arms and start crying while I'm trying to talk.

"Joey I missed you I needed you so bad so much happened this guy kidnapped me and Kevin came back and killed him now he's locked up for murder and this girl drugged me and I don't know where she is at."

"Just slow down baby calm down everything is going to be okay I'm here now and I'm not going to let you out of my sight let's just get home first and we will talk."

"Okay baby," I say while wiping my tears.

When we get home I tell Joey everything that happened while he was in the hospital expect for me and Kevin having sex I left that part out. Joey is stunned in shock not really knowing what to think.

"I'll handle this baby girl lets just enjoy each other for now I missed you," he says to me.

"Okay honey what do you want to eat I'll cook," I reply

"It doesn't matter anything you make is good to me."

"Thanks honey you're still sweet to me."

I make Joey some rice with gravy, baked chicken and sweet peas. We lay down after we eat and watch a movie. The movie turns into laughter which turns into touching which turns into kissing and the rest is history.

CHAPTER 8

We wake up to a loud thud in the front living room, Joey tells me to stay in the bed he will check it out but I'm to nervous, I don't want to be alone so I follow a couple steps behind him. A man in all black swings at Joeys with a bat, Joey takes the blow to his forearm and unleashes a fury of punches at the man after that. The man went stumbling back on the stove and Joey grabbed his head and started banging it against the stove and counter top. Two more men rush at Joey I start screaming and run to my phone to call 911 when I get in the room a girl in all black punches me and drag me by the hair back in the kitchen where the two other men are fighting Joey. They are getting the best of Joey for a while until he sees me screaming on the floor being dragged by my hair. Then it's almost like a second gear kicked in on Joey and he lifted one of the men above his head the second man was punching him in the gut but it had no effect on him. Then Joey kicked the second man in the chest while still holding the first man in the air. Then second man went flying across the kitchen floor and Joey slammed the first man on his knee and you could hear the crack of his back a mile away. Then Joey started pounding his face in with his fist. While he was doing that the girl and the second guy take off running.

"Joey their getting away," I scream

If I wouldn't have told him then I think he would've kept pounding that guys face in. Joey gets up with blood on his hands and face and it wasn't his blood. He takes off running after the others; I want to see so I rush to the window. He gets a hold of the girl first and throws her to the ground with remarkable force she doesn't move but I can hear her cry. The other guy is still running Joey catches up to him jumps on his back, the man falls face first. What Joey did next hurt even me, he grab the back of the man's head and slammed his face into the concrete repeatedly at least twenty times. He was half way down the middle of the street but I could see blood flowing all the way to the sidewalks. Joey walks back over to the girl and takes off her mask and look who that is, Amy I should've known, coming to seek revenge for a psychotic twisted lover pimp what ever he was to her. I call 911 I was too stunned to move before, Joey picks up Amy and brings her back in the house and throws her on the living room floor like a sack of dirty laundry. The police get there shortly after we tell them everything that happened and they put Amy and Joey both in cuffs.

"What are you doing his is the good guy he saved our lives," I say in shock

"Ma'am we have to take him in he killed three people with his bare hands that's manslaughter,"

"It was self defense they broke in my house and tried to kill us."

"If that's so then the judge will sort that out but I have to take him in ma'am"

"Don't worry baby girl I'll be okay," Joey says

"I'm going to get you out of there Joey I promise I love you baby."

They put Joey in the backseat and several hours after assessing the scene and taping up my house for evidence then they drive off with Joey and Amy. I go to my father's house because I'm not allowed back in my own house until forensics gets done. I get to my dad's house and tell him everything that happen my father is either too sleepy to respond emotionally or too much as happened lately and he has no emotion left.

"Let's get some rest dear it's late we will handle this in the morning."

"Okay dad sorry if I am putting to much stress on you."

"Your not angel I'm glad your safe though that's all I care about."

We both head to bed, the next morning we go to the jail to see about Joey's bond and his bond is set at 100,000 cash. Joey's mother gets there while we are leaving we tell here how much it is and she breaks down crying because she doesn't have 100,000 cash. How many people do now a days? My father comforts her for a while and invites her over the house for coffee she declines and goes home crying. I know she feels horrible her husband and only son have been taken away from her by the justice system, damn

JAHZAEVION "J CLIP" MOSLEY

justice system. I know she must feel pretty suicidal right now, I know I would if I were her. My father and I head home in silence I know we both have a lot on our minds though.

A couple days later they allow me back in my home but I don't even want to live there anymore after what took place there, my dad and Stacy help me find and move into a new apartment closer to my dad. I use to not want to live near my dad because I didn't want him check in up on me now all I want is for him to check up on me. Crazy how a couple events can change your whole out look on life. I continue to see Kevin and Joey, both in Jail. The two loves of my life are taken away from me both for murder and both murdered to protect me. How do I commit my heart to just one I feel like I owe them both my life. I go to court again a couple weeks later and the prosecutor drops the case he has no evidence I ever committed a crime, the ruling for the death of Zach Tucker was an accident due to car collision. That was great news but the least of my worries I wanted my boys back at least one of them. I go visit Kevin in jail, it's time for me to let one of them go I can't keep leading them both on.

"Hey baby you look like you gaining some weight in here," I say

"Yeah thanks to you baby doll for putting that money on my books every week they don't feed us shit in here," Kevin replies

"I want us to be together Kevin I will be here for you no matter what I love."

"I love you to baby I miss the hell out of you this place isn't for me I'm meant for the world I'm going crazy in here."

"Has anyone tired messing with you," I ask

"Of course not I'll beat one these dudes ass if they mess with me you know that girl," he replies

"Yeah I know baby just making sure you still got it and didn't go soft on me."

"Never that I'm still the man even in here I got a couple buddies in here with me from the street."

"Well aren't you right at home."

"Not really I need to get the hell out of here before I catch some more charges," he says

"What's wrong baby."

"These got damn guards think they tough as hell with that badge on and they disrespect all the inmates like we aren't shit but animals, they treat us inhumane in here baby."

"What happened tell me?"

"This one black guard keeps provoking me to kick his ass by saying little slick comments and the other white guard follows all the rules to the extreme and it's not even that serious dude. He be like don't eat while standing up, really guy I'm done eating I'm throwing my food away, no sit your ass down and finishing chewing. Like this is the type of bullshit I have to deal with in here totally uncalled for."

"Do not do anything stupid I'm going to get you out of here you didn't kill John Wilson and Nathan was in self defense don't worry baby you will be home soon." I say.

"What's going on with that Joey guy I seen on the news he isn't getting out because he murdered in cold blood because once they left the house self defense went out the window."

"I don't know," I reply

"Well I know a couple guys were telling me because they know some one who went through something similar before," he says

"I don't know I just hope you both get out because neither one of you deserve to be in here."

"Times up let's go," the guard yells

"I love you baby I'll come visit you next week," I say

"I love you to baby girl I'm go masturbate to your sexy face and juicy breast and thanks for wearing the shirt it really shows a lot of cleavage."

"Your crazy boy but I love you."

He walks out and I get up and leave I really miss the hell out of him what am I going to do with my life while he is gone.

I go to work the next day and a lot more guys try to talk to me since the seen me on the news and usually I would enjoy the attention but now I just want to be left alone. The next couple days are extremely hard for me I don't know how I am going to look Joey in them beautiful green eyes and tell him I don't want to be with him any more. His visit is coming up in two days and I don't know what to do. I call Stacy and ask her if she could get some weed for me I just need to be high right now I can't think. An hour later my doorbell rings it must be Stacy with the weed.

"Hey girl," I say as I open the door

"What's up ugly I got the goods," she says

"Thanks girl I really needed this I don't know how I am going to tell Joey I don't want to be with him any more."

"Girl you are lucky you got two great men that want to be with you, if you don't mind you could pass one to me I'm kind of single right now."

"Kind of single," I say

"Well my boyfriend right now isn't shit I would drop him in a hear beat for either Kevin or Joey."

"Girl you crazy I told you that's not cool I'm sure there not the only two good guys in the world."

"Your ugly and your being selfish don't you want to see my happy to," she replies with envy

"Of course I do where you are going with this I called you over here to get high and help me think not to add to my aggravation."

"Oh now I'm aggravating you what ever girl; you are so lucky and don't know what you got. You got two men that put there life on the line for you I can't even get my boyfriend to take out the trash. You're so selfish and your stringing both these guys along I hope they both leave you."

"You can just leave my house now I don't want to be around you right now," I say in awe

"I was already leaving and I don't want to be around you either, loose my number."

Stacy leaves my house and I really feel like shit now. I roll up and take the deepest inhales ever I am so I high I past out shortly after smoking.

It's time for me to go visit Joey and I am so worried about how he will respond I'm not sure if I will be able to handle it.

"Hey gorgeous you look beautiful in that dress you going somewhere when you leave here."

"No I just wanted to look cute for you," I reply

"Well you look more than cute baby girl you look immaculate," Joey says

"no I don't' stop making me blush," I say with the brightest, reddest cheeks ever

"I'm serious Anne thank you so much for coming to see me all these times and helping my mom with putting money on my books you been so wonderful to me I owe you much I promise I will not forget what you are doing for me it means so much."

He feels like he owes me after what he's I already done I owe him still I'm just trying to do whatever I can to repay him back, wow this guy really is amazing.

"Don't feel like that Joey you already did way more than enough for me it makes me feel good to be able to do whatever I can to help you."

"So how you been holding up out there is everything okay with you," he says

"Yeah I been okay I got a new apartment on the north side of town closer to my dad."

"That's good your fathers a good man I really like him I wouldn't mind calling him dad."

"You say that now until he shoves the bible down your throat."

"Ha-ha that's funny but I might need a little Word in my life, I'm sure it wouldn't be that bad," he replies

"Maybe I had some good moments in church as a kid it wasn't all bad how I make it seem."

"I know baby I really missed you though, every time you come visit me being in here doesn't feel so bad."

"Aw you're still the sweetest Joey."

I don't know how I am going to tell him I just want to be with Kevin and I don't think I can he is making it so hard for me.

"If I ever get out of here I'm going to marry you but I'm not expecting you to wait on me I know you have to move on with your life but if your single when I get out of here and you still want me I'll be on one knee with the biggest diamond ring I can find," says Joey

"Thank you Joey but you don't have to I'll love you no matter what and you will always be my friend."

"Times up let's go," the guard yells

"Thanks for stopping by and checking on me Anne I really appreciate you."

"Your welcome Joey and thank you for every thing see you later."

So much for telling him I wanted to be with Kevin huh I suck at this. I go home with so much on my mind I can't even think I take a week's vacation from work, unpaid vacation of course I don't work for Wall Street. I don't want to see any news reporters or guys trying to talk to me or Stacy. I did not leave the house at all during my unpaid vacation I just slept, ate, and cried. I don't know what to do with my life a year ago it was so perfect now everything is falling apart. I am so lost in time I forget to pay my light bill and my lights get caught off I don't really care I don't have much food in the fridge and I like the dark right now maybe reporters will stop coming to my door I light a candle in my bedroom and just lay down. A couple hours later I hear my door bell ring and a lot of lights and people outside my house what is really up with these reporters I thought the lights being off would make them not come and there a lot more outside then usual. The ringing continues then it goes from ringing to banging. Wow these reporters are getting more disrespectful by the day. I go open the door to yell at the reporters and tell them to get the hell off my porch. When I open the door Joey comes running in and he shuts the door behind him.

"Joey but how did you get out of jail what happened."

"That is the same thing I thought when they said I was released," he replies

"So you don't know why they let go," I ask

"I do now and I was shocked I still can't believe it I don't know what to think right now."

"Sit down Joey let me get you some water,"

He sits down in the dark and I get him some water and I bring the candle out the bedroom in to the living room. The reporters have the house surrounded I just see flashing camera's in the window, something really big must've happened. I sit down next to Joey and he looks more sad than excited.

"What happened at the jail Joey, tell me you look sad."

"When they released me they took me into a room and the F.B.I and this other guy were in there. I sit down and ask them what's this all about, and then the guy says he is my father. I didn't know what to say. He told me he saw his only son all over the news facing 15 years for manslaughter and he couldn't handle it. He said he called the F.B.I and made a deal with them if they let me go and drop all charges he would turn himself in. They accepted the deal he just wanted to see me one time face to face and they allowed him to. He told me how sorry he was for never being in me and my mothers life, and that I grew up to be a brave man and he's really proud of me, and that I have my fathers blood in me. I stood up went around the table and hugged him with all my might I didn't want to let him go the F.B.I and jail guards had to pull us apart. Then they took him away and let me go."

"Oh Joey," I didn't even know how to respond to what he just said or how comfort him. I just put my arms around him.

"That was my dad and they took him away from me again and this time forever, at least before I had hoped that I would see him again now I have none. That was my father that I meet today." Joey puts his face in his hands and cries harder than I ever heard a man cry in my life, movies included."

I don't know what to say or do I just want to cry myself but that would be selfish of me I have to be strong for Joey he needs me right now.

"Come on baby lets go lay down in the bed," I tell Joey.

Joey stops crying and wipes his face with his shirt such a guy. Then we go in the bed room and lay down in the dark.

"Why is the whole house dark," Joey asks.

"Listen the lights got cut off because I didn't pay the bill I just been so stressed lately."

"Its okay I still love even in the dark," he replies

"Baby how much you love me," I ask

"Baby girl my love for you goes further than the measure of time the light from the moon is the only thing I need at night to make an enchant full, pleasurable, breathe taking love with you," he says

"Yeah, well how bad do you want me?"

"Girl you know I want you more than satin wants Gods throne I feel for you every moment out of my day. The spiritual love bonds we have together grabs at my soul which causes me to get arouse, scream out loud and call your name. Baby I want you so bad that if you touched my lips right now you'll melt in my arms because of the fire on my tongue. Where every there's fire their water so you'll start to spill from your bosom drip down your silk thighs and cause my hardwood to jump high."

"I love when you talk to me like that tell me more, how would you handle this," I ask

"Like a crazed, wild, insane, untamed, animal I would tame it first by wipe lashing it a couple times with my tongue. Then I would pet it slow, fast, and gentle with my hands

After I would inject it with some type of formula to put it to sleep," he replies

"You are so poetic Joey I love it," I say

"I love you my queen," he replies with a kiss

We make love all night and forget about all our problems an events accruing in our life the only thing that matters is us and it feels good.

We wake up next morning feeling rejuvenated but we both still have a lot on our minds. For me it's how am I going to tell Kevin now that I'm with Joey and for Joey how is going to deal with meeting his father and is he going to keep contact with him while he is in the federal penitentiary. The first thing I need to do is pay this light bill I call the electric company and pay with my debit card over the phone.

"Hey bay I'm a go visit my mom she hasn't seen me since I was locked up she said she can't stand to see me behind bars so see only wrote me."

"Okay baby call me later I love you," I reply

"I love you to now it's time to duck and dodge these reporters I'm not ready to talk to them just yet."

"I know how you feel, how did you get here," I ask.

"I took a cab but I'm going to take the bus to my moms house my cars there she came over and picked it up while I was in jail right."

"Yeah she did but take my dads car I'm not going any where today."

"You sure bay."

"Yeah of course I don't want my man on the bus it makes me look bad," I slightly giggle.

"Thanks babes you're the best," he replies and kisses me before he walks out the door.

As soon as he opens the door a ton of reporters are waiting to swarm him I'm pretty sure Kevin is going to see him leaving my house, then again he doesn't know where my new apartment is at so I'm good for now. My heart can't let either one of them go I love them both equally in different ways, what am I going to do with myself? Later that night Joey comes back and I'm in the middle of dinner.

"Hey baby your back," I say

"Yeah sorry it took so long I gave the reporters a time of day so they could finally leave me alone. It smells good in here I see we got lights."

"Thanks and yeah I paid the bill and my dad picked my up so I could go grocery shopping."

"That's good because I'm hungry I'm ready to eat right now."

"You didn't eat while you were out baby," I ask

"Yeah I did but I'm so glad I'm not eating that jail food I just want to eat all the free world food."

"Free world that's what you call it," I laugh

"Ha-ha yeah it was a habit I picked up in jail everyone calls life outside of jail the free world," he replies

"That's cute and funny well don't worry baby your free world food will be done shortly,"

"Thank you beautiful."

We eat dinner and Joey loves my food he always loved my food but he really loves it now.

"Hey tomorrows Sunday right," Joey ask

"Yeah why," I reply

"I don't know I was just thinking of going to church do you want to go to your dads church."

"When did you get all holy on me Joey," I sarcastically say

"I'm not all holy I just thought it would be nice to show up at your dad's church after all he's done for us."

"Well we can go to church if you want but not my dads," I say

"Why not your dad's church what's wrong."

"Nothing but if we go to my dads church he's going to make our problems the center of his sermon and I hate when he does that."

"No I don't think he would do that," Joey replies

"You don't know my dad and yes he would do that he's been doing it my whole life that's one of the reason why I stopped going."

"Well what more can he put out that the news hasn't already told come on it won't be that bad."

"Ok I'll go just this one time just so you could see for yourself and maybe not want to go as much as I next time."

"Or we will like it and you will want to go as much as me next time," he replies

The next morning we get ready for church I haven't been to my dad's church since high school this should be interesting. When we get there my dad doesn't notice us yet the choir is singing and it sounds beautiful. That's one thing I do miss about church the choir and the songs they sang always brought peace to me. My dad is getting ready to go up and preach after enjoying the choir sing for about forty five minutes. When he stands up behind the pulpit we lock eyes and his face just lights up with joy, it made me smile to see him so happy. My father opens his bible and grabs the microphone.

"Glory to the God I serve He is a good one thank you Jesus. I'm just going to jump right into this I don't want to waste too much of your time we will be out of here shortly. If you have your bibles turn to '2 Samuel 11:2-5 One evening David got up from his bed and walked around on the roof of his palace. From the roof he saw a woman bathing. The woman was very beautiful, and David sent someone to find out about her. The man said, she is Bathsheba, the daughter of Eliam and wife of Uriah the Hittite. Then David sent messengers to get her. She came to him, and he slept with her. Then she went home. The woman conceived and sent word to David, saying, "I am pregnant."' Now David was the King of Israel and this was a time of war for Israel and in that time the king would be at battle with his troops but since David was out of place he was open to sin. That's what happens in our lives when we are not in proper place we give gateway to sin. God wants us positioned to do his will but if we are out of position we leave our selves vulnerable for the desires of the flesh. Now Uriah the Hittite was a faithful servant of King David and while David was sleeping with his wife not at battle but out of position, Uriah was at the battle fighting for his king's freedom. God didn't like this not one bit. David had wives and concubines and he decided to get pregnant his faithful servant's only wife who was at war for him. You could imagine how furiest God was at that time all because David was out of position. Had he had been in proper position in his life he could've avoided ever even seeing Bathsheba. Therefore he would have never been able to be tempted by her beauty and open the door for sin to over take him. We need to get into position it might cost our lives if we don't. David went even further than that he had Uriah killed in battle by placing in him on the front line. Sin opens doors to more sin. So David couldn't stop at just sleeping with his wife he had to get the man killed. That's what happens in our lives we do something we have no business doing and we try to get ourselves out of it by doing more stuff we have no business doing, digging ourselves deeper holes in sin. All David had to do was ask God give me ten more wives that look like Bathsheba and God would have blessed him with what he wanted. If we ask according to Gods will he will open the heavens to us. When we seek by our own knowledge it usually leads to failure and set backs. God wants us to need him that's why he puts us in situations to call on his name. We just have to open our mouths and call on the name Jesus. Skip to '2 Samuel 12:10 Now, therefore, the sword will never depart from your house, because you despised me and took the wife of Uriah the Hittite to be your own.' Now not only did David dig a deeper whole in sin for himself but he dug a deeper whole of sin for his family. The things we do in this life effect everyone around us who is apart of our lives. We may not attend for it but I'm sure David didn't attend for none of what was about to happen to his family to happen but it did, because he was out of place to begin with and gave way to sin. I'm not going to take up any more of your time just five more minutes, I advice you read the chapter when you get home though. God took David's son that Bathsheba gave birth to that's was one of the consequence for what he's done. Then year's later one of David's other son's Ammon raped his sister Tamar because he was madly in love with her. Then David's other son Absalom killed Ammon and it didn't stop there. So much grief happened to David because he was out of position. It's time to get in position saints we don't have time to waste. We are living in the last days and God is calling us to get in to position. Give all the praise to Jesus thank you Lord. At this time if anyone would like to give there life to God I advice you come down to alter so I can pray with you."

The choir starts lightly singing in the background and Joey does something I wasn't expecting, he walks down to alter and falls to his knees and screams out Jesus, Jesus save me God. The whole congregation rejoiced in joy and my father laid his hands on Joey's head and started praying for him. I was shocked and embarrassed at first then I was happy I had a man who wanted to give his life to God and I loved him even more for it. I walked down to alter and knelt beside Joey and my father placed one hand on me while the other on Joey. I felt more connected to Joey and my father then I ever had in my life and it is a bond I never want to break. Service was amazing and Joey was right I want to go back next Sunday just as much as he does. After church my dad, Joey and I go pick up Joey's mom and we go out to eat, it was a wonderful peaceful dinner at Oliver Garden everything felt so perfect and in position like my father would say.

The next couple of weeks couldn't have been better my life finally feels like it's getting back in order. Then I get a call from Kevin, why when things start going good something has to happen to complicate it.

"Hey baby they just released me from jail and dropped all the charges Amy told them everything and cleared my name," Kevin says

"Wow that's good to hear I'm glad for you," I say with no enthusiasm

"Come pick me up I'm ready to get home and make love all over the house," he replies

"Things changed Kevin I'm sorry I didn't tell you earlier I just didn't know how."

"Wait what are you talking about things changed," he says in a serious tone

"I'm in love with Joey and I'm with him now I'm so sorry Kevin please forgive me," I pled

"No forgive your self for breaking my heart," he says in anger

"I'm sorry but I can still pick you up and take you where you want to go."

"No I don't need you, you've done enough enjoy your life with out me," he hangs up.

Any other time I would've started crying but I don't, I'm happy I finally got that over with I love Joey and he is where my heart belongs. Come to find out Stacy picked up Kevin just like the back stabbing slut she is and then ended up together. I don't really care they deserve each other their both whores. Joey and I end up getting married a year later he proposes to me at Newport Beach in Rhode Island it was July and we just took a boat out on the sea and came back and had a beautiful candle light dinner on the dock. Later that night we go walking along the beach talking and laughing in the night light the ocean was so beautiful. Then he stops and I ask him what's wrong then he gets down on one knee and pulls out a gorgeous gold three karat diamond I was so shocked, stunned and excited all at the same time. Then he asked me 'Anne Marie Johnson will you take my last name and be my wife' hell yes is what I said and he put that beautiful ring on my finger and it looked even better on me. Joey takes us to Atlanta, Go for our honeymoon he said he doesn't want to have the conventional honeymoon at some resort he said he wants to get a hotel for a week and go to every club in the city. That's exactly what we did, we get a room at the W which was a club also and we club hopped and got drunk all week. We also ate at some beautiful restaurants like Benihanas in Buck Head and we ate at Papa Duex and Bahamas Breeze in Gwinnett County. We had the best time ever in Atlanta, GA I haven't seen so many clubs in my life they got more clubs then liquor stores. We got back to Worcester and bought us a house with the help of my dad and his mom. Come to find out before his father went on the run he left his mother 50,000 dollars and told her to give it to Joey when the time was right and I guess she felt the time was right. Joey gets a job working as a Bank Branch Manager and I get promoted to Mall Director. So much for Kevin and Stacy they end up breaking up because they were both whores who couldn't trust each other and when I got promoted to Mall Director I fired Stacy of course. I end up getting pregnant and if it's a boy we are going to name him Jack Joe Watts after Joey's father and if it's a girl we are going to name her Mary Ann Watts after my mother. I guess things worked out the way they were supposed to, all that I went through, who would've imagine two years ago that my life would end up like this. Joey and I laugh about it all the time when we first meet he was too passive to come on to me and I was to in love with Kevin to give him a chance. The fact that he was so passive is probable why he stayed my friend so long I kind of threw him in the friend department so I never looked at him like some one who would try to sleep with me. Can't say the same now he killed three people with his bare hands and took two bullets to the chest there isn't anything passive about him now and I love it. I am so happy my life couldn't be any better I have a wonderful, faithful, handsome, hardworking, best friend who so happens to be my husband. I am now Annemarie Watts, I have a father and a mother, and I will always remember who I'm loyal to.

Epilogue

Joey walks down a long bright cement hallway, the scent of disinfect and oranges in the air. Two guards are standing thirty feet down the hall from him, when he arrives at there location they let him into the visiting area. Joey sits down at the table closes to the window and waits with his arms folded and emotions in a knot. The anticipation of finally seeing his father for the first time craters through his atmosphere. Sweat drips under neath his shirt tickling his body with anxiety. A cold calm of winter chills his arms and goosebumps defend his comfort. So many questions, so many thoughts swarm Joeys head with a forceful impact, he starts to get a headache. He looks up when he hears the clink clank sound of the doors being unlocked and opened. A small short dark haired man with rough skin texture and the look of a man who worked the graveyard shift his whole life walks through the door.

"Stand up boy I gave my life up for you least you can do is stand up and shake my hand," his father says with great volume

Joey stands with a puddle of tears streaming down his face, this is such an unreal moment for him. He dreamed of the day when he would see his father, he had so many faces in his head about who or what his father would look like. He zeros in on his father n locks in eye contact, they both hold the moment. They can hear nothing but the throbbing of each others speeding heart beats; for so long this day has eluded them both. Now the time is upon them and it over whelms him; Joey runs to his father and the guards reach for there weapons until they realized what he was doing. He is bear hugging his father with his face buried in his fathers state uniform crying like he never cried before. He lets out years and years of pain and loneliness; his father is stunted with silence as Joey pours out his sorrows. His father was tense at Joeys reaction of seeing him then he relaxes and puts his arms around him; kisses him on top of his head and says, "I'm here son, I'm finally here."

After repeatedly being told to sit down by the guards they do and they sit and they stare and they each wait for the other to speak.

"Where do we start," Joey says with pain as if he was reading his own eulogy.

He is a very talented person who wants to display his gifts out in the open for the world to see. He has a sound track to go along with this novel on Itunes, Spotify, Etc. He is also an inspiring actor and comidenan. He loves his three beautiful children Lyric, Jaeanna, and Jayla and prides himself on being a dad that's his greatest joy. He just wants a chance to prove his talents to the world and provide a life for his children greater than his own upbringing.

He wrote this book because he has a vision for his life and people and this book is apart of that plan. He started writing this book in 2012 and all thought its been a long journey the finish product is finally here. Enjoy!

Instagram and Twitter @1JCLIP

LOYAL AFFECTION 2
WHITE SLAVES

The night was restless for Kevin he couldn't get any sleep. He knew how powerful of a impact he would have on history if he was successful. He decided to write his speech for when he address the public at the fund raiser, which is ways away but Kevin was a foreshadower by nature and leader by heart. He felt a heavy burden of hope drop on his shoulders and ran to his note pad and sighed aloud, "operation white slaves the first speech." He sat down at the table in front of him and began to write.

Thank you all for coming out today this is a very important day for our youth and their future. (Kevin imagined himself in a room full of superstar athletes from all sports, in the heart of the community.) some of you may ask yourself why did I choose this location, others maybe familiar with these types of locations. We are here because this is where your fans are; this is where the future is, where children with incredible talent and abilities are. Children with dreams and aspirations, who are motivated by the athletes in this very room. Because of the living standards and communities as a whole their resources and reach are limited. Should they not be given the same chance at success as any other middle class community in America. Congress is focused on the greater America which is the middle class, it is up to people like you and I in this room to focus on the weakest parts of America. I am asking now today that all athletes across the country and even caring people across the world. That you pledged to help me reach a goal of $300 billion dollars over the next 10 years. This money will be used to train low income communities in construction and positions involved in maintaining a stadium. Then we will have new stadiums built in low income communities by low income communities ran by low income communities. with the revenue stream pouring into the low income community; we can turn a low income communities into middle class communities. For the players sacrifice and commitment we have a shareholders program set up based on athletes performance and status. Which means no more owners taking 50% of your sweat and labor. Stadiums, marketing and salary cost will be paid by profits and the remaining profits will go to youth sports leagues constructed in same manner as professional leagues with proper stat tracking and the best medical treatment and rehabilitation. Also a universal league for each sport allowing children to travel and learn more about their country. I know most children who never leave the neighborhood and this will allow those without the means to travel to be able to. This will lift the hearts of the American people all across the country and will put the power and control into the hands of the players. I believe we can collectively reach a goal of $30 billion a year weather through donations or fund raisers. If your not able to use your wallet use your influence. But this is a reachable goal and we will change the face of sports in this country forever. Today is the first day of course altering history and for everyone who attended today you apart of it weather you act on it or not. Your placed will be marked in history regardless of your actions so why not capitalize and seize this moment of eternity. Every effort in your body should be towards this project and the future of your children's children. The mass wealth distribution being withheld from the low income communities is demeaning and we can change that and restore hope and structure. Some of you in this room have friends or family that could've made it professionally or collegiately if they had the resources at home. Because of poverty they turned to a life a crime or worked a job. They were not able to chase their dreams because of their living standards. If we elevate that standard who knows how many next great athletes and role models will come from it.

Kevin put the pen down in excitement at his own imagination. He knew it would be ways away before anyone would even hear that speech and he had a lot of work to do right away. He called his brother and cousin in Texas. it was easy enough for him to convince them to move in with him considering what they asked him before in past and he objected to the idea. Then he called his good friend from high school who moved to Pittsburgh, PA.

"Hello?" Drew says.

"My nigga what's popping boy." Kevin replies

"This my nigga Kev? Boy what's good how you been? I ain't heard from yo ass in a minute." Drew zealously says.

"It's been real; trying get some stuff lined up but I need you my nigga." Kevin replies with hesitation and seriousness in his voice.

"Bruh what's good you know I got you whatever you need." Drew replies immediately.

Kevin tells drew everything, his whole plan and stressing Drew's importance to not only to what he was what trying to accomplish but to Kevin himself. Kevin loved his family and all his close friends he considered family. He knew everyone had dreams of their own to pursue but he loved being with his family. He also knew if he in was a financial position to bring everyone closer they all would be willing. After talking with Drew they both decided to three-way friends Jah and Kah in providence. They were twins and their father lived in Worcester across the street from Kevin growing up. so when they came to see their father on the weekends they would play with Kevin and the other kids outside.

"Yo Drew" Kah answers the phone.

"Kah my nigga what's up boy this Kev we on three-way." Kevin shouts

"Kev o'l big head ass what up nigga." Kah replies

"Grinding you know, but I got a move I want you and Jah to be apart of. Where he at by the way?" Kevin replies

"He right hear I'm a put you on speaker phone." Kah says

"Nigga" Jah yells

"What's up boy" drew says

They all converse over the phone and everyone is on board. They are excited about Kevin's ideas, and plan to relocate to Kevin's house immediately. Over the next few days everyone is has arrived. Kevin, his brother and cousin, the twins and drew were all standing about in the kitchen.

I want S/O to
Clip N Kidd Ent
Official Threat Records
Floor Money Ent
Big Fraze
3rd Lane
New Money
Jenai
Hazel Octavia
Esiae & Mike Touze
Russel Ford Brown
Mr. Wincoop Of Times 2 Academy
02908
East Atlanta
Worcester
Rockford
Beloit
Houston
Juice Mobb
LA Lashes By BMaxx
Allah

CPSIA information can be obtained
at www.ICGtesting.com
Printed in the USA
BVHW081027150819
555975BV00001B/140/P